OHIO
DOMINICAN
UNIVERSITY™

SINCE 1911

Donated by
Floyd Dickman

The Spirit and Gilly Bucket

Also by Maurine F. Dahlberg

Play to the Angel

The Spirit and Gilly Bucket

MAURINE F. DAHLBERG

FARRAR, STRAUS AND GIROUX

NEW YORK

Copyright © 2002 by Maurine F. Dahlberg

All rights reserved

Distributed in Canada by Douglas & McIntyre Ltd.

Printed in the United States of America

Designed by Robbin Gourley

First edition, 2002

1 3 5 7 9 10 8 6 4 2

Library of Congress Cataloging-in-Publication Data

Dahlberg, Maurine F., date.

The spirit and Gilly Bucket / Maurine F. Dahlberg.— 1st ed.

p. cm.

Summary: In 1859, when Gilly's father goes to search for gold in the Rocky
Mountains, the eleven-year-old is sent to stay with her aunt and uncle in
Virginia, where she befriends one of her uncle's slave girls, finds out about
the Underground Railroad, and discovers that people are not always exactly as
they seem.

ISBN 0-374-31677-5

[1. Slavery—Fiction.   2. Underground railroad—Fiction.   3. Aunts—
Fiction.   4. Virginia—History—1775–1865—Fiction.]   I. Title.

PZ7.D15157 Sp 2002

[Fic]—dc21

2002022177

With love to my own "kinfolk":
Randy Dahlberg,
Myldred Fairchild,
and
Virginia Fairchild

And in loving memory
of
Frank Fairchild

The Spirit and Gilly Bucket

1

I WAS DREAMING I WAS HOME.

In the dream, I was sitting in front of Pa's and my little cabin. A redbird flew by, which everybody knows means good luck. And sure enough, just then Pa came running up, crying, "Gilly! Gilly! Look! I've found gold—right here in Katy Creek!" He dropped a pile of gleaming rocks at my feet. They nearly put my eyes out, they shone so bright.

"So now you don't have to go out West, after all!" I cried. We danced round and round. Somewhere in the distance, a fiddle played a perky tune.

Pa kept saying, "Gilly! Gilly!" but his voice slid up and up on the scale until it was high and soft. Then I was rising through layers of sleep, faster and faster, just the way I came up to the surface of Fox Lake after jumping in. I didn't want to come up, but I couldn't stop myself.

My almost-grownup cousin Sarah was smiling down at me. Her light-brown hair curled around her pretty face and over the shoulders of her red-checked dress.

"Gilly, I've called your name a dozen times! I told Mama you need to sleep late after making that long trip, but she says the servants have to start washing the dishes, so you'd better get up now if you want any breakfast. Papa has gone to Alexandria for a few days. Mama and Neddy and I are nearly through eating."

"Neddy?" I repeated sleepily.

"Your other cousin, my little brother."

"He's not a baby, is he?" For the past month I'd lived with a couple back home in Prairie Flower, the Cadwalladers, who'd made me take care of their howling, whining baby.

To my relief, Sarah replied, "He's seven. Didn't you know you had two cousins?"

I shook my head. I wouldn't even have known I had an *aunt*, except that I'd asked Pa once if he and I had any kinfolk, and he'd thought a minute and said, "Well, we don't have any on the Bucket side. On the Madison side there's your ma's sister, Laura. Orneriest dad-blamed woman in the state of Virginny."

Sarah grinned. "Well, you do have two cousins, and it's

time you got to know us. Now come *on*! I'll tell Mama you're on your way."

She ran downstairs. I kept lying there like a sack of flour. That dream had been so real! Why, I could swear I still heard the fiddle! But the only gold I saw was the handle of the white china pitcher on the washstand. And I wasn't in front of our cabin in Prairie Flower, Missouri. I was at Glencaren, Aunt Laura and Uncle Henry Hayden's wheat farm in Virginia, in a bedroom so fancy I bet even President Buchanan didn't have a nicer one.

And Pa was in a gold-mining camp in the Rocky Mountains.

Or was he? The familiar hot, scared feeling came over me. How did I know Pa was in the Rockies? How did I know he was still *alive*? He and his friend Rufus Peacock had left Prairie Flower in August 1858. Now it was April 1859. My last letter from him had come in January.

All the way from Prairie Flower, I'd hoped and dreamed there'd be a letter from Pa waiting for me at Glencaren. But when I'd asked Sarah last night, she'd shaken her head and said, "No, I'm afraid not. Maybe you'll get something this week. Papa will be back Thursday or Friday. He can go to the post office then if he hasn't already stopped on his way home."

"Mary Gillian Bucket! Do you want breakfast or not?"

Aunt Laura's voice could make a stone jump up and

run. My feet hit the floor, and I grabbed my old brown calico dress. It was filthy and stank of train soot, but I didn't have time to unpack my clean dress.

"Coming, Aunt Laura!"

I saw Aunt Laura in my mind: stout, with dark hair pulled back into a tight knot, hard black eyes, a little puckered-up mouth, and a nose that tilted up at the end. When I'd arrived the night before, she had looked me up and down without smiling and said, "So you're Mary Kate's girl, are you? I'm her sister, your aunt Laura. This is your cousin Sarah. She'll help you get settled while I go talk to Dr. Granger, our friend who brought you from the train station. By the way, you don't have fleas or lice, do you?"

"Why—no, ma'am!"

"Good. Our people work hard to keep out the vermin."

Sarah had been the one to make me feel welcome. She'd asked me all about my trip, and said I'd be like her little sister. She'd taken me to the outhouse (she'd said the polite name was the "necessary house") and waited while I went in. On our walk back, she'd pointed out the other outbuildings: the smokehouse, the dairy, the icehouse, and the small building that housed the kitchen and laundry.

As I'd followed her upstairs to the bedroom, she'd said, "You'll be sharing my room. I hope you don't mind sleeping in the trundle bed."

"I don't mind," I'd replied.

After the narrow plank on the hot, stinky train where I'd tried to sleep for two nights, the little bed that had been pulled out from under Sarah's big one had been heavenly. Even so, it had taken me hours to get to sleep. Finally I'd gotten up and stood at the window, looking out at the moonlit farmyard while I'd thought about Pa and wondered what my life here would be like.

I hadn't been the only person at Uncle Henry's who couldn't sleep. From a window over the kitchen and laundry, a thin white curtain had suddenly been pushed back at one corner, as if somebody was peeking out. I'd waved, but to my disappointment the curtain was then dropped quickly. This morning it still covered the window, and there was nobody in sight.

I buttoned my dress, stuck my red hair behind my ears, and was down the stairs before you could say skin-a-tadpole.

The dining room was on the right-hand side of the entry hall, behind the parlor. At the table sat Aunt Laura and Sarah and a little boy with curly light-brown hair like Sarah's. I guessed he was Neddy.

When I came in, they stopped eating and stared at me.

Aunt Laura murmured, "My word."

"Who's that?" Neddy gasped.

"This is your cousin Gilly from Missouri," Sarah said. "We told you she was coming, remember?" She hesitated,

7

then said to me in a kind tone, "This evening when the servants aren't so busy, I'll have them fill up the bathtub and you can take a bath. I'll do your hair if you like."

"I have another dress in my trunk," I said quickly. I guessed I did look a sight. I wasn't pretty, even at my best: I was small and skinny for an eleven-year-old, and had freckles all over my face. My red hair was so wiry and springy that Pa said it wouldn't lie down flat if a locomotive ran over it. Still, I should have at least run a comb through it and put on my cleaner dress.

"Go on and get some food." Aunt Laura made a scooting motion with her hand.

At first I thought I was supposed to fix my own breakfast, the way I did at home. But Aunt Laura had waved toward the marble-topped sideboard. I went over and lifted the lid of the big pewter serving dish that sat there. Hot, steaming bacon, scrambled eggs, and potatoes were waiting for me. My mouth watered. All I'd gotten to eat on the trip was train-stop food: stringy meat, cold beans, stale bread, and mush. And I'd always had to gobble it because we'd never known how long the train would be at the station. The couple I'd traveled with, the Kansas cousins of the Cadwalladers, had been fussy and nervous. They'd tugged on my arm and cried, "Hurry, we'll be left behind!" every time I'd tried to take more than two bites of anything.

I filled my plate and took an empty chair beside Neddy. Sarah poured a glass of milk from a pitcher on the table and put it in front of me.

"Where's Missouri?" Neddy asked.

"Out West." The potatoes, fried with onions and spices, were the tastiest things I'd ever eaten. I'd have to learn how to make them so I could surprise Pa when we—if we—no, *when* we got home.

"Are there Indians?" Neddy wanted to know.

I swallowed my mouthful of potatoes and said, "Yes, lots! Every night they'd come around our cabin with their tomahawks, yelling and screaming. Why, just a few months ago—"

"That's nonsense, Mary Gillian," Aunt Laura said firmly. "There haven't been any Indian uprisings in your area for years."

"Well, not *many*."

"Not *any*."

"Yes, ma'am." She was right, of course, but she shouldn't have ruined my story.

Then Neddy wanted to know why my hair was cut short, and it didn't seem very interesting to say that I'd chopped it off last summer because I'd gotten hot and it was too thick and springy to braid. So I told him a big old bear had bitten it off. He stared and Sarah smiled.

Aunt Laura snorted. "Mary Gillian, I think that will be enough," she said.

But Neddy asked, "How come you're going to live with us?"

"*Ned*dy," Sarah protested. "Let your poor cousin eat her breakfast."

"It's okay," I told her, and turned to Neddy. "I won't be living with you for very long. See, my pa went out West to find gold. But he isn't going to *stay* out West. Once he's rich, he'll go back to Missouri and send for me. I was supposed to stay there with a friend, Granny Pea, who was taking care of me while he was gone."

"Granny *Pea*." Neddy giggled.

"It's short for Peacock. Her son Rufus went out West with Pa. I called her Granny because—well, she was like my own grandma. But she died of a heart spell real sudden one night, a couple of months ago."

I pictured Granny Pea: tall and gaunt, with a craggy face, a pipe in her mouth, and gray eyes that could have stared down an Indian chief. I missed her so much. Even now, after two months, it was hard to believe she was gone.

"Then what happened?" Neddy prompted.

I took several bites of scrambled eggs before I answered.

"Some neighbors, the Cadwalladers, took me in. They found your ma's name and address on some letters she'd written to *my* ma, and wrote to her. Your ma and pa said I could stay here until my pa gets home—which will be any

10

day now," I added, flashing a look at Aunt Laura. "The Cadwalladers had cousins from Kansas who were coming to visit kinfolk in Washington. I call them the Kansas Cadwalladers. They brought me on the train to Washington, and I came the rest of the way all by myself."

I hoped Neddy would ask more about that, so I could tell him how brave I had been. Once, when the train braked to a sudden stop, the other passengers had screamed, but I hadn't.

"Mary Gillian," said Aunt Laura, "I hope you remembered to thank Dr. Granger. It was nice of him to fetch you on his way home from town."

"Yes, ma'am, I thanked him."

I'd liked quiet, friendly Dr. Granger. He had reddish hair that was sort of like Pa's, kind eyes, and a gentle voice. I'd told him I'd learned all about herbs and remedies from Granny Pea, and we'd compared recipes.

"Where's your mama?" Neddy wanted to know.

"She died five years ago," I replied. "There was a cholera epidemic, and lots of people died. I was sick, too, but I got well. Pa says I'm as strong as an ox."

"Did your mama look like Mama?"

That question caught me by surprise. My pretty, dainty ma look like stout, pinch-faced Aunt Laura?

"Well, yes, sort of," I lied. "Look, here's something that used to be Ma's."

I reached under my dress bodice and pulled out the

pendant that hung around my neck. It was made like a forget-me-not flower, with a cluster of white seed pearls forming the center and five pale blue enamel petals around it, in a gold setting. It was the thing I was fondest of in the world.

To my surprise, Aunt Laura gasped. "That's Mary Kate's forget-me-not!"

I smiled and said, "Yes, ma'am. Pa gave it to me when she died, and I've worn it ever since. Do you want to see it?"

I started to get up.

"No!" she snapped, as if I'd offered her a dead frog. "I've seen it plenty of times. It belonged to our great-aunt when we were girls, and Mary Kate took such a liking to it that Great-Aunt Berta finally gave it to her. Hmmph! I never had any use for such gewgaws myself."

My pendant was hardly a mere gewgaw! But before I could say so to Aunt Laura, the outside door opened and a young black woman came in. She looked a few years older than Sarah, and was tall and slender, with very black skin. She wore a neat cotton dress, and her hair was tucked under a red kerchief.

"May I take the breakfast things now, Miz Hayden?" she asked quietly.

"Yes, Clio." Aunt Laura nodded.

I watched Clio clear the table and the sideboard. She worked quickly and gracefully, as though she'd had a lot of experience.

Neddy wasn't finished asking me questions. "Do you miss your ma?"

"Yes. I miss her and my pa and Granny Pea."

"Aren't you scared something will happen to your pa?"

"Neddy, what a question!" Sarah cried.

"I'm not worried about Pa." I tossed my hair. "He's the bravest man in the world. Why, once he strangled a big old rattlesnake with his bare hands! He could even wrestle a—"

"That's *enough*, Mary Gillian," said my aunt.

Sarah said quickly, "Gilly, after breakfast we can go upstairs and get out some of my old dresses for you to try on. Won't that be fun?"

"Of course," I said politely. But I didn't want to try on dresses. I wanted to go outside and give my legs a good run.

To my relief, Aunt Laura said, "Sarah, you're forgetting that you have to go to Miss Jenny's for your own dress fittings this morning. I'll give Jupiter a pass to leave the farm, so he can drive you. Mary Gillian, you'll be expected to help Clio with the housework, but Josie, our laundress, said she'll do it this morning. She's been doing it lately because we've been shorthanded. That means you'll have a few hours to get settled. Then this afternoon you'll help Clio and me make candles."

She stood up. "I'll be out in my herb room all morning, preparing my spring tonic and several other remedies that Dr. Granger wants to purchase."

"I can help you!" I told her, excited. "Granny Pea was an expert on remedies, and she taught me all about them. I know how to—"

Aunt Laura was shaking her head firmly. "I use my own secret recipes. Besides, I don't let anyone help me except Tolliver."

"Tolliver?"

"He's the old cook," Sarah explained. "He helps Mama with her herbs. Her herb room is upstairs over the kitchen and laundry."

"I saw somebody up there last night," I said.

Aunt Laura looked at me. "What are you talking about, Mary Gillian?"

I shrugged. "I couldn't sleep, so I got up to look out the window. The white curtain at one of the upstairs windows moved. I figured somebody was looking out, so I waved. They didn't wave back, though."

"That's because there was no one there," my aunt said. "Nobody goes into my herb room at night."

"But I'm certain—" I started.

Aunt Laura wasn't listening. "Sarah, you'd better get ready to go," she said. "I'll tell Jupiter to bring the buggy around. Neddy, you help Carter gather the eggs. Mary Gillian, try to stay out of trouble."

I glowered and scuffed my feet as I went up to my bedroom. I *had* seen that curtain move, no matter what Aunt Laura said. Besides, why wouldn't she at least give me a chance to help her make remedies? Herbal remedies were my specialty. Granny Pea had been known all over eastern Missouri for her knowledge of cures, and she'd let me be her apprentice. I knew which plants were best for what ailments and how to make everything from teas to syrups. Granny Pea had taught me *her* secret recipes, and they were probably lots better than Aunt Laura's.

I changed into my other dress, which was a faded red-and-blue plaid, and hung my dirty brown one on a hook because I didn't know where else to put it. My two night-gowns and unmentionables went into the bureau drawer Sarah had cleared for me. They were all I had to put away. Someone had brought my trunk upstairs, but it could go to the attic without being unpacked. There was nothing in it I was likely to need. Mostly it held Pa's and my few remaining valuables: his fiddle, our silver candlesticks, the Bucket family Bible, and several quilts Ma had made.

I looked out the back window. You could see a thousand times farther through these glass windowpanes than you could through the greased paper that had covered our windows at home. In the distance, I saw woods that looked far enough away to give me a good run. Once I'd reached them, I could sit in the cool greenness for a spell.

I decided I'd better move quietly as I left the house. I didn't know whether Aunt Laura's idea of staying out of trouble included running off into the woods.

If I hadn't been trying to tiptoe silently down the front

stairs, I might not have heard Aunt Laura's voice coming from the dining room.

". . . can't believe she was wearing Mary Kate's pendant! Imagine, a valuable heirloom like that around the neck of a dirty little frontier girl!"

I wasn't dirty! I thought angrily. I did have some train dirt on me, but I couldn't help that.

"Now, Mama." That was Sarah's voice. I couldn't hear what else she said, but her tone was gentle.

"Well, I suppose it could be worse," Aunt Laura grumbled. "At least that no-account pa of hers didn't gamble it away, like he did everything else. I had a letter from that nice Mr. and Mrs. Cadwallader who kept her. They said her pa lost all his money gambling. He even had to sell his blacksmith shop to pay his debts! That's why he had to head for the mountains."

"It's not Gilly's fault," came Sarah's voice again.

"I'm not saying it is, Sarah. I always knew Gil Bucket was a no-good scoundrel, even before he dragged my poor sister out to the frontier. And *now* look at him—abandoning his child to go pan for gold. Well, Henry and I'll raise her because she's Mary Kate's daughter, not because I have any sympathy for that pa of hers."

I ran out the front door, through the yard, and all the way to the back woods. But I didn't run joyously, as I'd planned. I wanted to get as far as I could from those hurtful words. I raced past outbuildings and a cluster of little cabins, into the woods. Brambles tore at my arms, vines caught around my ankles, and sobs came up from deep inside me.

Finally I came to a creek. It was a poor little thing, not nearly as big as Katy Creek back home, which the people of Prairie Flower had named for Ma when she died. Still, it spoke the same language. Its quiet bubbling and splashing comforted my heart. I dropped down beside it.

Aunt Laura's words still rang in my ears: *that no-account pa of hers . . . abandoning his child . . .* How *dare* she say those things about Pa? And dang-blast those prissy Cadwalladers! They hadn't had any right to tell her and Uncle Henry the rumors about Pa's gambling. He *was* fond of gambling, but he never bet more than he could afford to lose. The reason he'd had to sell his little blacksmith shop and go West was that his money had been stolen. He'd told me so! That adventuresome Rufus Peacock had been telling him for months that the two of them should go West and seek their fortunes—and after the theft of his money, which I didn't really understand, Pa had finally agreed to go.

I pictured Pa the day he left, tall and straight, clean-shaven, his red hair hanging to his shoulders and his blue eyes looking straight into mine. I heard him say, "You take care of yourself and don't fret about me. I'll be back as quick as I can."

"I know you will," I'd said. I'd swallowed the lump in

my throat and tried to grin. "And I'll bet we'll be rich as lords with all the gold you'll bring home."

He'd grinned back. Then he and big old black-bearded Rufus had ridden away.

Now nobody knew where they were. Some other men from our area who had gone out to Pikes Peak had come home in March. They'd said nobody had heard from Pa or Rufus since the two of them had left the main camp to strike out on their own in early February.

But Pa'd be back. He'd *promised* he would be.

I imagined him riding up to Uncle Henry's farm, bags of gold hanging from his saddle. He'd scoop me up and we'd ride away. We'd build us a mansion in Prairie Flower. And I'd write to Aunt Laura. "You can come visit us," I'd say. "Just be sure you pick off your fleas and lice first."

Finally I sobbed myself out.

I wiped the tears off my face with my sleeve, then got up and walked along the creek. I expected it to peter out shortly, but then up ahead I saw a broad clearing and a great silver expanse of water. That little tiny creek ran into the Potomac River!

The Potomac was prettier than the Mississippi or the Ohio, which the train had crossed on our way here. Those rivers had been fearsome things, wide and muddy brown. This was a smaller, silver-blue river that invited you to have picnics beside it.

I climbed into a big sycamore tree on the bank and

edged out along a thick limb until I was sitting over the river itself. I sat there for a long time, listening to the water lap against the land below and watching distant geese bob up and down on the ripples. The sunshine peeked through the tree leaves and warmed me, but the gentle breeze coming off the water kept me from getting sweaty and drowsy.

While I sat there, I thought—maybe harder than I'd ever thought before. When I finally climbed down the tree and started back to the house, I felt able to face Aunt Laura again. Not because I'd forgiven her for her words, but because I'd made a decision.

She and Uncle Henry wouldn't have to raise me. I would stay here for two months, until the middle of June. That would give me time to get some supplies together and work out a plan. Then if Pa still hadn't sent for me, I would leave this place and run off to Pikes Peak to find him.

2

WHEN I GOT BACK, I went up to the attic and took some paper and Pa's pen and ink from my trunk. I sat on the floor and made a list of what I had to do before I ran away.

1. Find out how to get to the Rockies.
2. Figure out how to get away from here without getting caught.
3. See what grows in these parts to use for food and cures.
4. Gather knife, matches, blanket, poncho, ax, kettle, spoon, and so on.
5. Think up story to tell people I meet along the way.
6. Get money and food to take!!!

I underlined "money" three times. I would need to have some to pay for emergencies and for ferries across rivers. But the only money I had was a dollar bill that Rufus Peacock had once given me to play with. Pa had said it was what was called "wildcat money," because the bank that issued it had gone broke. He'd laughed and said, "You can play with it, but if you go trying to spend it you'll get thrown in the calaboose!"

I wasn't sure what a calaboose was, but I was pretty sure I didn't want to get thrown into one.

I put my finished list in the trunk. There certainly was a lot to do before I could set out to find Pa. But, I told myself, I had courage and determination. Granny Pea had always said you could do just about anything if you had courage and determination.

Before I went downstairs for dinner, I washed my face and dragged a comb through my hair. I wouldn't have Aunt Laura thinking Buckets were dirty. I also lifted my pendant outside my bodice, so my aunt would have to look at it.

I made myself be quiet and courteous all through dinner. What I wanted to do was scream at Aunt Laura, tell her how wrong she was about Pa and how mean she was to say the things she'd said about him. But I knew if I did, she'd say, "See? I was right. Gil Bucket hasn't raised his daughter to be fit for civilized society."

While we were tucking into our macaroni, Neddy

asked, "Gilly, will you tell me stories about wrestling bears and wild Indians?"

I hesitated, then replied, "If it's all right with your ma."

Aunt Laura looked surprised and smiled a tad. "I suppose it won't hurt. But it'll have to wait until after the candle-making. And please don't make your stories *too* bloodthirsty, Mary Gillian."

"Oh, I won't, ma'am," I said, giving her my best innocent look.

The candle-making operation was set up in the back yard. Granny Pea and I had always used candle molds, which made enough for both her and Rufus's cabin and Pa's and my cabin. But Aunt Laura had prepared a big kettle of tallow and tied rows of wicks onto long rods. She showed me how to take a rod of the hanging wicks and dip them, all at the same time, into the kettle. Then we'd lay each rod across two poles that rested on chair backs, so the forming candles could cool. We'd have to go back and dip the rods again and again until the candles were big enough.

By late afternoon, we'd made enough candles to light up all of Prairie Flower for about ten years. My back ached from bending to dip the wicks, and my fingers were burned where the hot tallow had splashed onto them.

"How come we need so many candles?" I asked Clio.

" 'Cause they be for Miz Sarah's new home as well as

for the big house and the cabins here," she replied, stirring the tallow.

"Sarah's new home?"

"Yes'm, didn't you know? She be gettin' married the first of June."

I pondered that as I dipped the remaining wicks. I was sorry that my kind cousin would be leaving so soon. But, I reminded myself, I'd be leaving just a couple of weeks after her—even sooner, if Pa sent for me.

I wanted to ask Aunt Laura more about Sarah's upcoming marriage, but I was determined not to speak to her except to say "Yes, ma'am" when she gave me directions about the candles.

At supper I tried to be aloof and eat slowly, even though we were having a chicken pudding that was so good I wished I could gobble. I made sure I held my fork properly, too, so Aunt Laura wouldn't think that Pa and I ate everything with our knives like *some* frontier folks (Rufus Peacock, for instance).

Afterward, while we were leaving the dining room, my aunt said, "Mary Gillian, you've been very subdued all day. You're not feeling peaked, are you?"

"No, ma'am."

She looked at me thoughtfully. "I'd better give you some castor oil, just in case."

So all I got in return for acting civilized was a dose of the worst-tasting stuff anybody had ever invented.

That evening, Sarah took me out to the laundry room for my first-ever bath outside of a creek or a lake. While I undressed, she filled a round tin tub with water that had been heated over the fire.

"You're sure nobody will come in from the kitchen?" I didn't mind Sarah seeing me undressed, but I remembered that Glencaren's cook was a man, Tolliver, and I didn't want him barging in while I was wearing only my skin.

"I'm sure. Come on, get in!"

I climbed into the tub and sat down. The water came up over my chest. It felt nice and warm—like sitting in Katy Creek when the sun had been shining on the water all day.

Sarah gave me a cake of soap to lather myself with, then sat down on a three-legged stool beside me so she could scrub my back.

"Do those stone steps go up to Aunt Laura's herb room?" I asked.

"Yes, it's overhead."

I frowned. "I really did see a curtain move up there. It wasn't my imagination. But why would anybody be in an herb room in the dark?"

"Maybe it was Josie's ghosts," Sarah replied lightly.

"Josie's *ghosts*?"

"Umm-hmm. Old Josie the laundress says she's heard thumping and crying overhead when she's been in here at night. She thinks it's ghosts."

"Do you believe her?"

Sarah laughed. "No. Josie's very superstitious, like a lot of old folks. Now, lift up your hair so I can wash behind your ears."

I bunched up my thick, springy hair and held it.

"Granny Pea was old, but she didn't believe in ghosts," I said. "She said that even if you're *sure* you see a ghost, it's always just an animal or a white sheet or something."

"She must have been a sensible woman," Sarah said. "At any rate, I'm sure Mama wouldn't let a ghost into her herb room. She doesn't let anybody go up there except Tolliver, Clio, and Dr. Granger."

"Why not?"

"She says she wants it to stay clean and tidy."

"Have you ever been up there?"

"Once or twice, a long time ago," Sarah said. "Mama's the herbalist, not me."

"Does she keep it locked?"

"No, it's an open attic. The only thing that's locked is a storage room, where she keeps her expensive store-bought herbs and the remedies she has ready to sell. But don't you think about going up those stairs! If Mama ever catches you in her herb room, she'll skin you alive. Now, let's wash your hair."

I'd never dreamed that looking pretty took so much work! First, Sarah scrubbed my hair with soap and rinsed it with clean water. Then she got a couple of eggs from the kitchen, beat the whites into a froth, and painted my hair with them. After that, she smeared butter on my lips. Finally she covered my face with a mixture she said was made of powdered pumpkin and cucumber seeds and milk.

I felt like something good to eat. Gilly cake, I thought, then giggled. "I bet if somebody came in and saw me now, they'd run!"

"This is nothing compared to what I'll have to do before my wedding day," Sarah said.

She pulled strands of my hair, stiff with froth, so that they stuck out straight.

"Who are you marrying?" I asked.

"His name is David Thurmond. He's from New York, but he moved down here a few years ago. A lot of young men from New York moved here, because they could buy worn-out tobacco fields for nearly nothing and turn them into good farmland. David bought an old tobacco plantation about ten miles from here. He had to work hard to improve the land, but now it's a fine wheat farm."

"How did you meet him?"

"His sister Olivia was a friend of mine at Coombe Cottage, the school in Fairfax Court House where I went."

"Fairfax Court House!" I said. "That's where Ma and Aunt Laura grew up."

Sarah nodded. "That's right. Grandpa Madison had a

beautiful house. I remember visiting it before he and Grandma died. Anyway, David came to our graduation exercises. We started courting, and last winter he asked for my hand. I was afraid Papa'd say no, because David—well, he thinks differently from Papa and Mama. But they like him anyway, and Papa said yes."

She picked up a bottle of dark liquid. "I'll wash the egg out of your hair now."

"With *rum*?" I squealed, looking at the bottle's label.

Sarah laughed. "Yes! It keeps your hair clean and makes it grow faster."

After my hair was rinsed and the paste taken off my face, I stood up while Sarah poured rinse water over me. Then I dried myself, put on my dress, and followed her up to our bedroom. I sat at the dressing table while she brushed my hair. It took a long time for her to get out all the knots. She tried to be careful, but it hurt and I said "Ow!" a lot. I even used a few cuss words, which made Sarah blush and say, "*Gilly*, wherever did you learn such language?"

I grinned. "Mostly from Rufus Peacock. Pa says he has the biggest heart in the world, but he'll always be as rough as an old coyote. Even his ma gave up on teaching him any manners."

When my hair was as nice as it was going to get, I tried on some of Sarah's old dresses. Two of them fit me: a green one and a white, blue-sprigged one. They were a little big in the bodice, but that just made them more comfortable.

"Mama gave your old brown calico to Josie to wash," Sarah told me. "Monday is usually laundry day, but Josie was sick, so she's going to wash tomorrow."

At bedtime, Sarah covered my face with a wheat-bran mix that she said I had to keep on overnight. She also gave me a store-bought toothbrush, which truly *was* easier to use than my finger or a twig.

The next morning, I had to admit that I looked better—and smelled better, too—after all that Sarah had done to me. When I went downstairs wearing the old green dress of hers, even Aunt Laura nodded in approval.

"I guess you'll do," she said grudgingly. "I only wish you had your ma's hair—long, thick, dark hair it was, smooth as silk. It's too bad you didn't inherit it."

She didn't say, *instead of your pa's ornery red hair*, but I knew that was what she was thinking.

I followed Clio around and learned how to make the beds and do the other household chores properly—which meant the way Aunt Laura liked them. It would have been less burdensome if Clio had been chattier, but she was the most silent person I'd ever known. At home, Granny Pea and I always sang and talked while we did the housework.

After I'd made the beds and opened the windows, Aunt Laura told me to dust the parlor and Uncle Henry's library, which was across the hall from it. That fit right in with my plans, because I wanted to see whether the library had an atlas. Pa had had one, with maps of America and foreign countries. He'd shown it to me once, but all I remembered was that the smudges were mountains and the lines were rivers and Missouri was as far west as you could get before the territories began. Now, though, in order to do number one on my list—"Find out how to get to the Rockies"—I needed to study a map of America.

Uncle Henry's atlas was a big, red leather-bound book that opened stiffly, as if it hadn't been used often. I found the map I needed. My heart sank when I saw the distance between Virginia and the Rocky Mountains.

I couldn't possibly walk all that way alone! Maybe I could just try to get back to Missouri, then find some people to travel on West with—*nice* people, not like the Kansas Cadwalladers. But, looking at the map, I could see that even walking from here to Missouri would be a trial.

Still, I couldn't give up this soon, not when I was just on number one of my list. Courage and determination, I thought.

A voice behind me said, "What'cha looking at, Gilly?"

I jumped like a big old bullfrog, but it was just Neddy.

"You said you'd tell me about your life in Missouri. Are there lions and tigers?"

"Oh, all over the place! Why, you can't even go to the

out—I mean, to the necessary house—without having one pounce on you. Come sit down and I'll tell you about it."

I was afraid that if I didn't dream up some stories for him, he might go to Aunt Laura and say I'd been looking at that atlas. Besides, I liked the way his eyes got wide with admiration when I talked about Missouri. Nobody'd ever looked at me that way before.

I decided to tell Neddy enough hair-raising stories to give him nightmares for a week. While I was in the middle of one about Pa and me fighting off man-eating sharks in Fox Lake while tigers waited hungrily for us onshore, Clio came in and swept the rugs. She worked slowly, and I wondered whether she was listening to me.

"Clio's one of our people," Neddy said when my story was finished.

"Our people?"

Neddy nodded and said, as though it was a lesson he'd learned by heart, "Our people work in the fields and in the house. We give them cabins to live in and food to eat. We don't overwork them and we seldom whip them. They work best if you treat them kindly but firmly."

He added, "Sometimes Papa lets me hand out their rations on Sundays. There's Carter and Nancy—they're Isaac and Dilsey's children. We play together, and I help Carter gather the eggs. Isaac, Dilsey, Zeke, and Daniel work in the fields. Josie and Jupiter used to work in the fields, but they're too old now. Josie does the laundry and spins cloth.

Jupiter works in the yard and drives us places. He plays the fiddle, too."

Jupiter must be the fiddler I'd heard my first morning here, when I was dreaming I was home with Pa.

"Mammy Evie was our mammy, but she got old and died," Neddy continued. "Tolliver's the cook, and Clio and Patsy work in the house. No, wait—Patsy ran off."

"Ran off?"

Neddy nodded. "Papa's in Alexandria buying a new slave. He and Mr. Craikey from down the road went together. Some of Mr. Craikey's people ran off, too."

"And nobody ever found them?"

He shook his head. "No. Mr. Craikey and Pa went all the way up to Baltimore to look. They even took Mr. Craikey's slave-catching dogs along."

"His slave-catching *dogs*?" I repeated, horrified.

"Um-hmm. They're killer bloodhounds that are trained to find runaway slaves. But they couldn't find Patsy and the others. Papa says the Spirit must have gotten them."

He said "the Spirit" with a sort of awe, the way you'd say "the President" or "the Holy Ghost." As if it was a particular being, not just any old spirit.

"What's the Spirit?" I asked.

He shrugged. "I don't know. That's just what grownups say when some of our people are missing—that maybe the Spirit got them."

"But is it—"

"I don't *know*. Tell me another story! Have bears this time."

So I made up a whopping great story about Pa and me fighting bears. I made sure I talked loudly enough that Clio could hear me. Maybe Patsy had been her friend, and a good bear-wrestling story would cheer her up.

Finally Neddy got his fill of stories, and went outside to play with Carter. I had been hankering to take a walk through the herb garden, and I figured I'd better do it now, before Aunt Laura got my days all planned out for me.

That garden was exactly what Granny Pea and I had dreamed of having: an old-fashioned one with a yew hedge around it and a stone path through it. A pink-budding crab apple tree stood right inside the entrance. Under it grew boneset. I nodded in approval. A tea made of boneset tasted nearly as bad as castor oil, but was good for relieving the aches and pains of the ague or influenza.

I walked slowly along the path. With all these herbs, you could cure *any*thing. You could even cure diseases no-body'd thought of yet! I stopped here and there, and rubbed the leaves between my fingers so I could sniff the familiar smells: lemon balm, sweet woodruff, queen of the meadow, spearmint, peppermint, feverfew, bee balm, clary sage, chamomile, rosemary, sweet marjoram. Some scents were as soothing as a sunset, others as spicy as

Christmas. I ran out of fingers before the garden ran out of herbs, so all their fragrances blended on my hands.

Lavender bushes sat in the corners by the gates. I stretched out my hand and touched a tall, budding spike. Lavender had always been Granny Pea's and my favorite herb. Just sweeping your hand through its spikes and breathing in the fresh, sweet smell made you feel better about life.

"Hey! What you doin' with them plants? You get away from there!"

A skinny old stooped-over black man was striding toward me, shaking a long wooden stirring spoon in the air. "Go on now, shoo! Them be Miz Hayden's plants, and she don't allow nobody but me to touch 'em! You hear me, missy?"

"I was just looking," I said indignantly. "Are you Tolliver?"

"That be my name, an' I seen you touchin' that lavender." His red-rimmed old eyes blazed at me. "You trot along now, 'fore I tell Miz Hayden on you. Shoo!"

"Mean as a swarm of wasps," I muttered, giving him a dark look. I did as he said, though. I didn't want that spoon walloping my backside.

I'd hoped I could spend the afternoon in the woods, but while we were eating our dinner of oyster soup and corn bread, Aunt Laura looked at me thoughtfully and said, "I don't suppose you can sew, can you?"

"Granny Pea taught me to sew and embroider and knit," I said proudly.

Aunt Laura nodded. "Good. This afternoon you can do some mending. If your stitching is good, you can help hem the sheets and pillow slips for Sarah's wedding chest."

Maybe, I thought, if I made my stitches big and crooked, she'd let me go outside instead. But once I started sewing, pride got the better of me and I did my best. When Aunt Laura looked at my work, she raised her eyebrows in surprise.

"Amazingly nice," she murmured, seeing my tiny, even stitches. "After you finish the mending, I'll give you some linens to hem. From now on, you can mend and sew in the afternoons unless you're needed to help with other chores."

I groaned.

After a while, Sarah came into the parlor and sat down next to me. Her job was a little more fun than mine, since she was embroidering pillow slips. But even that looked boring, because they all had the same old pink rose on them. I vowed that if I ever got married, I'd have bright-colored flowers on my pillow slips: red geraniums, yellow brown-eyed Susans, and deep purple violets. Each pillow slip would have a different flower. One would have a blue forget-me-not, I decided, patting the pendant under my bodice. I smiled, remembering how Aunt Laura had told

Sarah it was a valuable heirloom. I bet she wished it was hers and had called it a gewgaw because she was jealous.

"Thank you for helping us, Gilly," Sarah said. "There's a ton of linens to sew, as well as the everyday mending."

"You will be a help," Aunt Laura admitted. "We used to have a girl named Patsy who sewed well, but she—well, she's gone now. Josie used to sew, but her eyes are giving out. I suppose it's too much to hope that this new house girl Henry's buying will be good at needlework."

She frowned at Sarah. "I know what you're thinking, that we should hire workers instead of buying slaves."

"You know David doesn't believe in slavery, like you and Papa do."

No wonder Sarah'd been afraid Uncle Henry wouldn't let her marry David! Slavery was a big thing to disagree on. I glanced at my cousin, but her head was bent over her embroidery hoop and her brown curls hid most of her face.

We worked silently for a while. If all the stitches I'd made since dinnertime were stretched out in a line, I thought, they'd reach clear back to Prairie Flower.

Finally Aunt Laura folded her pillow slip and stood up. "I'd better go make the rounds of the cabins. I told Dilsey I'd take her children some tonic, and I need to dose some of the other people for coughs and such."

"I can help you!" I said eagerly.

"No, you keep on with your sewing," my aunt replied. After she'd gone, Sarah gave a long sigh.

"I don't know what I'm going to do, Gilly," she said. "I love David dearly. But like I told you, he's from the North and he thinks differently from most folks here, especially about slavery. He's gotten me to see his side—that slavery is wrong and should be stopped."

"That's what Pa says! There aren't any slaves in Prairie Flower, but Missouri's a slave state. Pa's always hated that. He says it's shameful and sinful for one human being to own another one."

"I'm glad he feels that way," Sarah said. She hesitated. "David thinks there's going to be a war soon, between North and South. Not just over slavery, but for other reasons, too. He says that if that happens, he'll take me to live with his family in New York and go fight for the North."

"But Uncle Henry—"

"Will fight for the South."

That possibility was so awful, I didn't know what to say. I mused on it as I mended one of Neddy's shirts. How could there be a war between parts of the same country? And how could kinfolk who both cared for Sarah fight on opposite sides?

I had wondered what my life here at Glencaren would be like, and by Friday night I thought I knew. Friday had been pretty much a repetition of Thursday: eat breakfast, help Clio in the house, eat dinner, sew linens and mend clothes, eat supper, play a little while with Neddy, go to bed. And all the time, try not to think about the awful things that could have happened to Pa.

I was nearly asleep when Uncle Henry came home. I lay very still so I could hear his and Aunt Laura's voices from the front hall.

"I sent the new girl down to Clio's cabin to live," Uncle Henry said. His voice was deep and gravelly, and sounded tired. "Her name's Lizzy or Tizzy or some such nonsense. She's been a field hand on a plantation near Richmond and doesn't have any experience in a house. Still, she speaks fairly good English and she's presentable. Has good teeth and no brands or whip marks. Says she knows how to do the laundry and ironing. I think she'll be okay, with some training. By the way, Simon Craikey's men gave up on finding Patsy and the others. He said they went clear up to Pennsylvania and didn't find a trace of them."

"That's unfortunate," Aunt Laura said.

Uncle Henry grunted. "We still figure that *Spirit* got hold of them. He probably got them a ticket on the underground railroad."

The Spirit again! I thought. And an underground railroad? How could a railroad run underground?

Aunt Laura said, "Clio will make sure the new girl is decently clothed and knows what's expected of her. She can start tomorrow morning, in the kitchen. Clio, Tol-liver, and I will watch and see how she does."

"If she isn't suitable," Uncle Henry replied, "Simon Craikey will buy her from me. He saw her this afternoon, after I'd bought her. He took a liking to her and offered to buy her from me right then, but I was starting home and didn't have time to go bid on another house girl."

Their voices drifted off into the parlor.

Before I went to sleep, I said a little prayer for the new house girl. No matter what her name was or what she was like, I didn't want her getting sold to a man who owned slave-chasing bloodhounds.

3

I MET MY UNCLE THE NEXT MORNING as we went into the dining room for breakfast. He looked much older than Aunt Laura and was thickset, plain, and stodgy. He had a heavy mustache and long sideburns. His hair was the color of a river otter and parted in the middle. It was slicked down flat, but he hadn't used bear grease on it, the way men did in Prairie Flower. Whatever he'd put on his hair smelled better than bear grease, although I guessed most things did.

When we met, he said, "Good morning, Gilly. I'm your uncle Henry. I trust you're getting settled in?"

I replied, "Yes, thank you. Did you bring the mail?"

He looked startled. I guessed it had been rude of me to

ask him that right off, but I had to know whether there was a letter from Pa.

"Why, yes, I did," my uncle said, "it's on the table in the front hall. That's where I always put it. I'll show you after breakfast."

"Was there a letter for me?"

He shook his head. "No. There was a letter for your aunt Laura from an old friend of hers, and the rest were bills." He chuckled. "You can have the bills if you like."

"No, thank you." I tried to smile at his joke, but I wanted to cry. I'd so counted on hearing from Pa today!

Uncle Henry could eat more than anybody I'd ever known, except maybe Rufus Peacock. He had at least three full plates of eggs, sausage, and potatoes, and half a dozen biscuits with quince preserves. They weren't little biscuits, either. They were what people at home called "cat's-head biscuits," because they were as big as a cat's head.

Between bites, Uncle Henry asked me questions. "How many folks live in Prairie Flower?"

"There are eight families besides Pa and me," I replied.

"Is there a school?"

I shook my head. "No, but I never needed one. Pa taught me to read and write and do sums. He's book-learned, you know, and very smart." I looked hard at Aunt Laura. "His friend Rufus Peacock taught me to fish and to read animal tracks. Rufus's ma, Granny Pea, taught me to sew and do housework and make cures."

"Isn't there a doctor?"

"Yes, sir. But even he used to send a lot of folks to Granny Pea. He said she had a gift for healing. She could get rid of warts by rubbing her *hand* over them!"

Aunt Laura cleared her throat. "Mary Gillian, we don't discuss warts at the table."

"Yes, ma'am."

We ate quietly for a minute. Then Uncle Henry asked, "Why did your pa decide to look for gold in the Rockies? I thought California was the best place to find gold."

"Rufus Peacock had been wanting to go out to California to look for gold, but Pa kept saying no because he didn't want to leave *me*." I gave Aunt Laura another meaningful look. "Then Rufus heard that a bunch of men from Missouri were going to Pikes Peak, which is closer than California. They said there were veins of gold there that had just been discovered and that if you got out there fast enough, you could take away all the gold you could carry. Pa still said no, but then all his money got—got stolen."

"Stolen?" Uncle Henry's fork stopped in midair. "How?"

I felt everyone's eyes on me. It was so quiet I could hear the big clock in the parlor ticking.

"I—I don't rightly know all the details. Pa came home

one night and said his money had been stolen by a—" I stopped. I didn't want my aunt and uncle to know that Pa ever said the kind of words he'd used that night. "By a *thief*. That's why Pa had to sell everything and go to the Rockies to hunt for gold. If that thief hadn't come along, we'd both still be at home in Prairie Flower."

Aunt Laura and Uncle Henry gave each other a funny look. I could tell they didn't believe me about Pa's money being stolen. They thought Pa'd had to sell his little blacksmith shop to pay his gambling debts.

I felt my face grow red with anger and humiliation. What made it worse was that I didn't understand myself how Pa's money had been stolen. When I'd asked him, he'd just said, "There's a lot of thieving, deceiving skunks in this world, Gilly-girl. But don't you go fretting about it. I'll put things to rights."

Sarah said, "Your pa must be a brave man to go out to the Rockies."

"He is," I said proudly, grateful to her for saying that. "He could whip his weight in wildcats!"

I was afraid Uncle Henry would ask when Pa had last written me. But Clio was coming into the dining room, and he was more interested in food than he was in Pa.

"There any more biscuits?" he asked, turning to look at her.

"Yessuh. The new gal, Rissy, is bringin' 'em."

The new house girl came in the door just then. She looked about my age. She was pretty, with glossy chestnut skin and widely spaced brown eyes. Her hair was tucked under a brightly printed kerchief, and she was wearing—

"My dress!" I hollered, pointing. "That girl's wearing my dress!"

The girl shot me a terrified look, dropped the silver platter of biscuits onto the floor, and ran out of the room.

"Clio, pick those biscuits up and throw them away!" Aunt Laura snapped. "Neddy, stop laughing. Look at what you've done now, Mary Gillian!"

"But she was wearing my *dress*. The brown calico one from home."

"I gave it to her," said my aunt. "It was too ragged for you to wear anymore."

She turned to Uncle Henry. "I caught that new girl stealing a piece of sausage off the plate when she brought it in. Getting set to stuff it in her greedy little mouth, she was."

Uncle Henry sighed. "Like I told you, she's been a field hand and doesn't know how to behave in the house. Clio and Tolliver will teach her better manners."

"Gilly," Sarah said quietly, "that poor girl probably thought you were accusing her of stealing your dress. Perhaps you should find her and tell her you're sorry."

"I will," I said.

Uncle Henry pushed his chair back from the table and stood up. "I'm going out to the cornfield. Want to come, Gilly?"

"Yes, sir!"

"Okay. Be ready at eight. Jupiter will bring the buggy around to the back porch."

"When you get back," Neddy said, "tell me how your pa whipped the wildcats."

Aunt Laura frowned at him. "When Mary Gillian gets back, she'll do her chores. Storytelling will have to wait."

"I'll tell you about the wildcats tonight," I promised Neddy.

I lagged behind while everybody else left the room. As I passed by the sideboard, I swiftly wrapped the last two pieces of sausage in my table napkin and put them in my pocket. Then I went out back to wait for Jupiter. It was only a quarter to eight, but I figured the new house girl might come along.

I was right. She soon came out of the kitchen.

When she saw me, she gasped. "I didn't steal your dress, miss, honest!"

"I know," I said. "I'm sorry I yelled. I was surprised because I'd never seen anybody else wearing my clothes before. Aunt Laura should have told me she was giving you that dress."

"Yes'm." She looked worried. "You don't want it back, do you?"

"No, it's yours now." I looked her over. "It looks better on you anyway, since you've got curves and I'm straight as a stick."

I took the sausage out of my pocket.

"Here, I brought you these. I wanted to bring more, but Uncle Henry ate like an ox. There wasn't much left after he got done."

Rissy looked longingly at the food I held out, but shook her head. "I ain't allowed to take food that's for the house. Miz Hayden done scolded me already for thinkin' nobody'd miss a li'l old piece of that sausage."

"I'll keep an eye out for Aunt Laura," I told her. "Go on, take it."

She ate the sausage as if she was starving.

"Thank you, miss!" she said afterward. "This mornin' was just hoecakes. In town, they fed us good at the slave pen, but I was too full of misery to eat."

I had a terrible thought. "You weren't separated from your family, were you? At the sale?"

She shook her head. "My mama died of sickness last fall. And my daddy—" She looked around to make sure nobody else was listening, then said in a low voice, "My daddy up and run off North last year. He was gonna send for Mama and me, but we never heard from him. He don't know Mama's dead, and he won't know where I am now. I fret over him somethin' awful, miss."

"I fret over my pa, too!" I said, excited. "He's out West

looking for gold, and I should have heard from him by now. My ma died of sickness like yours, except a long time ago. What's your name?"

"Mama named me Clarissa Ruth, but folks call me Rissy."

"I'm Mary Gillian, and folks call me Gilly. Not Miz Gilly," I added, "and not miss or ma'am. Just Gilly."

"Yes'm, Miz—I mean, Gilly."

"How old are you?" I asked her.

"I don't rightly know. I was born in the summertime."

"I was born in the summertime, too! July eighteenth. You can share my birthday if you'd like. We can both turn twelve. Although you might be older, since you're curvier. Would you rather be older?"

"No. I'll turn twelve, same as you."

We grinned at each other.

The kitchen door opened. Tolliver stomped out. "What you doin' out here, new gal? You want me to tell Miz Hayden you be socializin' when you got work to do?"

"I gotta go," Rissy whispered to me.

I grabbed her hand. "Can I come visit you sometime?"

Rissy thought. "Come out to Clio's and my cabin tonight after supper. I'll wash the dishes as quick as I can."

Tolliver scowled at me before he went back into the

kitchen. I knew he was mad because I was talking to Rissy. But she and I were going to be friends, whether he liked it or not.

A buggy, hitched to a pretty bay horse, came up to the back porch. The driver had white hair and skin the color of strong black coffee.

"You must be Jupiter," I said. "I like hearing you play the fiddle. My pa plays, too. Hearing you makes me homesick, but I like listening anyway."

"Thank you, miss," he replied, smiling.

Uncle Henry came out the back door. "You can go now, Jupiter. I'll drive."

As we made our way down a dirt path into the corn and wheat fields, my uncle talked about his farming methods. He used words I didn't understand: "nitrogen," "acidity," "marl," "plaster," and "guano." One thing was clear, though. "You're awfully proud of Glencaren," I said.

He looked pleased. "That I am, Mary Gillian. My daddy and granddaddy used this land to grow tobacco. After a while, it wore out from years of over-planting. Most of the land around here did."

I put in, "Sarah said David got his land because it was worn-out and being sold."

"A lot of people sold their land to New Yorkers. But I was born and raised here and wasn't about to give up. I swallowed my pride and learned new farming methods from those Northerners. They have funny ideas about slavery and such, but they do know how to farm. This year, for instance, I'm following their advice and using the best Peruvian guano to fertilize. It cost me sixty dollars a ton, but the wheat ought to bring in ten or fifteen dollars an acre when it's harvested."

He nodded toward two black men who were guiding an ox-driven plow in the cornfield up ahead. "There's some of my people working.

"Hey there, Isaac and Daniel!" he called.

The men straightened up, tipped their hats, and grinned. "Mornin', Mas' Hayden!"

"You boys getting set to plant some good corn?" Uncle Henry asked.

"Yessuh!" The shorter man grinned even more broadly. "We workin' *hard*!"

"You better be working hard, Isaac, you old rascal, you!" Uncle Henry laughed.

The men laughed, too.

As we drove on, Uncle Henry said, "They like it when I josh with them."

We caught up with two more workers, hoeing: a young woman and a very dark old man with grizzled gray hair. I guessed they were Dilsey and Zeke. A tiny girl clung to Dilsey's legs and watched us.

"Hey, Zeke, you aren't loafing, are you?" Uncle Henry called jovially. "Dilsey, haven't you got little Nancy working on her own yet? What, and her all of two years old? You all are planting me a good crop, aren't you?"

"Yes, Mas' Hayden!"

"We gets you the best corn you ever seen, Mas' Hayden!"

"You better," my uncle said, smiling. He clucked to the horse and we went on.

I looked back. Nancy was crying openly now, and Dilsey bent to give her a quick hug. I heard her say, "Them folks is leavin', honey. They won't hurt you none." Zeke wiped his brow with the back of his arm, arched his back to get the cricks out, and went back to hoeing. He was pretty old, I thought, to be working all day under the hot sun.

I wasn't sure why, but suddenly I felt embarrassed by Uncle Henry's joshing.

After my uncle had shown me the crops, he drove me around to see his animals: fawn-colored dairy cows, a small herd of sheep, and big brown hogs. They all looked healthy, and the barn and pigsty were sturdy and clean.

"Barn roof's new, just put on last year," my uncle said. "Cost a fortune, but I wanted the best. The cows are Alderneys. They're good cattle. They're small and don't eat much, but they give plenty of good, rich cream and butter. That's important because your aunt Laura makes extra butter to sell. She makes and sells cheese, too."

"She does?" Maybe I could help her, I thought. It would be better than sewing.

"It's a very nice farm," I told Uncle Henry.

"Thank you, Gilly. I work hard to keep it that way."

When we got back to the house, I spoke to Aunt Laura. "Uncle Henry said you make cheese and butter to sell. I can help you. I helped Granny Pea make cheese and butter lots of times. I know how to make rennet for the cheese with crushed thistle flowers, and how to hang the cheese in a pine tree to age."

"I use calf rennet and age my cheese in the dairy," my aunt said. But then she considered a moment and added, "Still, now that the new house girl is here, perhaps you could help. Judging from your sewing, you've been well trained in the domestic arts."

"Yes, ma'am." I grinned. Even churning butter would be more fun than making beds and dusting.

After dinner, I did my mending while Aunt Laura and Sarah sat on the sofa and pored over the latest *Godey's Lady's Book* fashion journals. The clothes they spoke of could have been from a storybook: ashes-of-roses silk, lilac brocade, fawn cashmere, embroidered cambric, claret silk with ivory lace trim. Deep flounces, looped pearls, tulle ruches, lace rosettes, fluted frills. I didn't know what all those things were, but I loved the sounds of the words. Lucky Sarah! It might even be worth getting married, to have finery like that.

My aunt said, "Sarah, did I tell you I had a letter from Emma Bussy this morning? She's going to be here for the months of May and June, visiting her kinfolk."

Sarah's face lit up. "That's wonderful! She'll come to my wedding, won't she?"

"I'm sure she will. My, it will be nice to see Emma again. We were the best of friends when we were girls."

"It's too bad she lives in Richmond now, so you don't get to see each other often," Sarah said. She turned a page of the *Godey's* and jabbed a finger at the picture on it. "Mama, look at this dress. 'Lilac silk shot with black, and satin borders on the flounces. Full undersleeves of white figured Brussels net.' Isn't it lovely?"

Lilac silk. Flounces. Brussels net. I sighed dreamily. "Aunt Laura, can I have a new dress for Sarah's wedding?"

"There won't be time to have one made," Aunt Laura said. "I'm afraid you'll have to make do with an old dress of Sarah's."

Sarah winked at me. "Don't worry, Gilly. I have some beautiful dresses up in the attic that I've outgrown. We'll find something pretty for you."

I smiled at her for being so kind.

That evening, I wanted to take Rissy some more food, but we had boiled eel with parsley sauce for supper, and I could hardly put a boiled eel in my pocket. I didn't even want to put that slick, oily-looking thing into my *mouth*.

"Nothing better than a boiled eel!" Uncle Henry declared happily. He pulled back the napkin covering the bread basket and peered in. "I don't care for these little French rolls, though. I like good, hearty bread."

He turned to Rissy, who was standing in the doorway. "Have you got any more of those potato buns, like we had for dinner?"

Rissy nodded. "Yessir. I'll go fetch them."

But a few minutes after she'd left, Clio came into the dining room empty-handed. "I'm sorry, Mas' Hayden," she said. "Rissy said you wanted tater buns, but there ain't no more."

"Oh, the Devil." Uncle Henry sighed. "Never mind. I'll make do with the French rolls."

I thought that for a man who could eat a nasty old eel with such gusto, he was being awfully particular about his bread. I could hardly keep from making faces as I swallowed my own eel, and I heard Neddy go *eeeuch* under his breath as he bit into his.

At least dessert was good: rich, sweet vanilla ice cream and soft, sugary fairy cookies. When nobody was looking, I stuck some of the cookies in my pockets for Rissy and me to eat later.

When I left the house, big piles of heavy white clouds were moving in from the west, and a breeze cooled the back of my neck. I bet it was going to rain before morning.

I had passed the Negroes' quarters when I'd gone to and from the woods, but this was the first time I'd come calling. Six cabins faced each other, with a dirt yard in between. They looked tidy and cared for, but even the largest one, which sat at the far end of one row, was smaller than Pa's and my cabin in Prairie Flower and not as nice. They didn't have greased paper covering the window holes, as we did, or front porches. Rufus Peacock, who was a carpenter by trade, had built us a wide porch. That was where I'd shell peas and strip dried herb leaves off their stems, and sometimes on summer evenings Pa and I would sit out there for a spell, on the split-bottom chairs Rufus had made us. Sometimes we'd talk and sometimes we'd just count lightning bugs.

Rissy was sitting on the ground outside the end cabin on my right, her arms wrapped around her knees. She was staring at the eastern sky, which the clouds hadn't yet covered, but she looked over when she saw me coming.

"Old Josie came and finished up the dishes," she said. "She felt sorry for me, it being my first day and all."

"What were you watching the sky for?" I asked. "Falling stars?"

"No, miss."

"What then, *miss*?"

Rissy grinned and ducked her head shyly. I sat down beside her.

"I'm watchin' for the first star to come out," she said.

"There's a real bright one that comes out before all the others. Back where I used to live, it'd come out over the barn. I don't know where it'll show itself here at Mas' Hayden's."

"What do you do, make wishes on it?"

"No, miss—I mean, Gilly. I use it to send my love to my daddy." She looked at me anxiously. "You think that's foolish, sendin' my love by a star?"

"Of course not! Tell me how you do it."

"Well, I use that first star 'cause it gets so bright I reckon Daddy'll see it in Canada or anywhere else he might be, and it's so high up, it can see all over the world and find him. So every night 'cept when it's cloudy, I watch for it to come out and I whisper, 'Give my love to Daddy,' and I close my eyes and think on him real hard. Then I feel better, almost like I just hugged him and said 'I love you' in his own ear."

"That's a fine idea!" I cried. "I'm going to send my love to my pa, too. I can find another star if you want."

Rissy considered that. "You can use the same one. It's so big and bright, I reckon it can find both our daddies."

We ate our fairy cookies while we waited for the star to come out.

"These are mighty tasty." Rissy sighed blissfully. "That Tolliver sure can bake, I'll say that for him."

She thought a moment. "Speakin' of Tolliver, it was real funny about them tater buns."

"You mean the ones Uncle Henry wanted?"

Rissy nodded. "I told Mas' Hayden there was more 'cause I'd *seen* 'em, sittin' in a basket in the kitchen not long before suppertime. But when I went to get some for Mas' Hayden, the basket was gone. I asked Tolliver where the buns were, and he swore there hadn't been any left from dinner. But I know there were—half a dozen or so."

"Maybe Josie's ghost got them," I said. I told her about seeing that white curtain move and about Sarah saying Josie thought there was a ghost in the herb room.

"You're sayin' there's a ghost livin' right overhead of where I *work*?" Rissy cried.

"Oh, there's no such thing as ghosts," I scoffed. "Sarah said that a lot of old people like Josie believe in them, but I don't, and neither did my friend Granny Pea back in Missouri."

"You do what you want, but I'm gonna find me a ghost charm to wear around my neck." Rissy shuddered. "Ugh, I don't like to think on ghosts. Let's talk about something else or I'll have nightmares tonight."

We talked about what our lives had been like before we'd come to Uncle Henry's farm. When I told Rissy about Prairie Flower, I didn't put in bears and tigers and wild Indians the way I did with Neddy. I told her about

Granny Pea and me working in the garden, and about Pa taking me for walks and telling me stories at bedtime, and about how he'd bring me little wildflowers and funny-looking rocks he'd found.

Rissy had lived on a big tobacco plantation in southern Virginia. Her master had had to sell her and some of his other slaves to make money because he'd had a bad crop.

"Mas' and Miz Percy wasn't so bad," she said, "but they had an overseer, Mas' Ellicott, who'd as soon whup us as look at us. I was lucky. He didn't pay much attention to a li'l gal like me. Mama was the laundress and didn't work in the field, so she stayed clear of him. My daddy had it hard, though. Mas' Ellicott whupped him all the time. Daddy finally told Mama and me he was leavin' for Canada. It about broke my heart. He was like your pa, playin' with me and bringin' me flowers. He taught me things, too. He even started teachin' me my ABC's. Oh!"

She covered her hand with her mouth.

"It's okay. I won't tell," I promised her. I knew that slaves weren't allowed to learn to read and write.

I whispered, "I'll help you! I can borrow one of Neddy's primers."

Rissy shook her head. "There's nothin' I'd like better, but if we got caught, you'd be in trouble, too, for teachin' me."

I thought about that. What was that thing Pa'd said lawbreakers got thrown into? A calaboose? But I'd have to risk it. *Every*body ought to know how to read and write.

"We won't get caught," I said firmly. "We'll find a place in the woods where nobody'll see us. We'll have fun!"

Rissy's eyes shone. "If you're sure you're willin' to teach me, I'm willin' to learn. Daddy left just as I was startin' to put letters together and figure out words. Mama didn't know how to read, and she didn't want me learnin' for fear I'd get in trouble."

"I'm sure I'm willing to do it," I told her. I turned my face upward. "Is that star out yet?"

Rissy scanned the sky. "There it is!"

My eyes followed where she was pointing. A tiny light appeared and grew brighter as I watched. It reminded me of a newborn calf, wobbling on its shaky legs and finally standing steady and sure.

Rissy said, "You ready to send our loves?"

I nodded. We both stared at the star and thought about our daddies.

"Send my love to Daddy," Rissy whispered.

"Send my love to Pa," I whispered.

We closed our eyes. I thought on Pa, felt my arms around him and my face against his rough jacket. I smelled the smell of the blacksmith forge, which always clung to him. I heard him say, "Take care of yourself, Gilly-girl." When I opened my eyes, I did feel as if I'd hugged him. He'd felt it, too, wherever he was. I was certain of that.

4

I'D FIGURED SURELY I could spend most of Saturday in the woods, but those clouds I'd seen kept crawling eastward until they covered the sky. During the night it began to rain. It wasn't any little piddle-plop rain, either, but the kind of downpour you could only go out in if you were a fish. The rain fell all day Saturday, and the wind whipped itself into a gale that blew down fences and ripped off tree branches. Uncle Henry said a million times how smart he'd been to have that new roof put on the barn.

Neddy and I watched out the window for a while, then played Snip-Snap-Snorum and Mixed Pickles on the parlor rug. He and Sarah had more games than I'd ever known existed: Pope and Pagan, the Jolly Game of Goose, the Mansion of Happiness, the Railroad Game, and Sociable Snake, as well as the two we played.

The next day, everything was muddy and soggy, but because it was Easter Sunday, Aunt Laura insisted we go to church.

Since it was Sunday, we had waffles with syrup for breakfast. I wanted to savor them, but Aunt Laura was almost as bad as Mrs. Kansas Cadwallader when it came to hurrying a body who was trying to eat.

"Look alive, Mary Gillian," she said. "Sarah and your uncle finished eating long ago and are upstairs getting ready for church. Neddy and I are done, too. We have to leave in fifteen minutes. You don't want to make us late, do you?"

"No, ma'am."

Neddy set down his milk glass and looked at me reproachfully. "You promised to tell me about your papa whipping wildcats, but you didn't."

"I'm sorry, Neddy. I will when I have time."

"You'll do no such thing," Aunt Laura said firmly. "After church on Sundays we read and write letters or pay visits. We do *not* tell crude, violent stories to one another. Now *hurry*, Mary Gillian. And, for goodness' sakes, put on some shoes and comb your hair. You look like a little heathen."

"Yes, ma'am."

After she left, I told Neddy, "You'll hear about the

wildcats tomorrow. And," I added, getting an idea, "I'll even show you the wildcat money that Pa and I got as a reward for whipping them!"

"Honest?" Neddy gasped.

"Sure. It's upstairs in my trunk." I figured I might as well get *some* use out of that wildcat dollar Rufus Peacock had given me, even if it was only to entertain my cousin.

I went upstairs, combed my hair, and stuck my feet into my shoes. Sarah found a hair bow that matched my blue-sprigged dress and pinned it on top of my head. But when I got downstairs, I could tell from Aunt Laura's expression that now I looked like a little heathen wearing shoes and a hair bow.

Jupiter drove us to church in the buggy. Tolliver rode with us, but the rest of "our people," as Uncle Henry called them, walked behind. The men wore trousers, starched shirts, and shoes. The women were a feast for the eyes in their pretty, bright-colored dresses. Some even had hoops in their skirts, and many wore jewelry. They all had either crisp kerchiefs on their heads or ribbons in their hair. Rissy was wearing my brown calico dress and had her hair in braids, tied with yellow ribbons that matched the dress's tiny flowers.

Uncle Henry looked at them and shook his head. "I don't understand why those women always waste their money on baubles."

Sarah replied, "They earn the money honestly by

working on Sundays and holidays. Besides, the cast-off dresses we've given them haven't cost them anything. And Clio says they make dyes out of berries and skirt hoops out of grapevines. So all they've bought is a few little trinkets."

My aunt said, "Maybe so, but your father's right. It *is* amazing how they spend so much of their time and money on frippery and gewgaws."

Neddy liked the rhythm that made. He sang, "Frippery and gew-gaws, frip-pery and gew-gaws," until Uncle Henry told him to stop.

While Aunt Laura had her head turned, I took my pendant out from under my bodice and hung it on the outside where she'd see it. It was one gewgaw I bet she wished was hers.

As we got closer, I could hear the church bells ringing. "Those bells sound like Pa's hammer hitting the anvil!" I cried. Then I wished I hadn't said it, because my aunt and uncle exchanged that same look they had when I'd talked about Pa's money being stolen.

The church was pretty, with its delicate steeple and arched glass windows. Inside, it was hot, and the pews were as hard and straight as train seats. I'd hoped I could sit by Neddy, so that if things got too boring we could nudge each other and bump our feet together. But the men and boys sat on one side and the women and girls sat on the other. The black folks sat in the back.

The preacher was old and almost as small as I was and

wore little spectacles. His white hair was so fine it looked as if he had milkweed fluff stuck all over his head.

He wasn't frail when it came to describing the pains of hellfire for those who didn't repent. He waved his arms and jumped up and down from excitement. But he didn't scare me: Pa had told me that I'd go to heaven and find Ma there, waiting for me.

The only part of the service I liked was singing the hymns. I heard a girl's voice soaring above the rest, and turned to see whose it was. Other people were looking, too.

"Face forward, Mary Gillian," my aunt muttered.

"But I want to see who's singing!" I hissed.

It was Rissy! I never would have dreamed that her voice had such power and beauty.

Finally the service was over, and we could step out into the fresh air again.

"Gilly," said Sarah, "I'm going to take Neddy out to the necessary house. We'll be back in a few minutes."

I saw Rissy with the other blacks and ran over to talk to her. "You didn't tell me you could sing like that!" I cried.

Rissy grinned and looked shyly at the ground. "We used to sing in the tobacco fields to make the time go faster. I've been scared to let loose and sing since I got here, for fear Miz Hayden or Tolliver might get mad. But at church, I reckon I can sing as loud as I want. Only thing is, I have to hum when I don't know the words."

I started to say, *Soon you'll be able to read them,* but I stopped myself. Somebody might hear me. Besides, even when she did know how to read, she'd have to keep it a secret.

"Come on, Rissy," Clio said. "Time to be startin' home."

Rissy quickly said, "I gotta work till after dinner, Gilly, but come down around candle-lightin' time and we'll look for our star."

"Okay. Wait a minute, and I'll go ask if I can walk home with you."

I ran back to where my aunt and uncle were chatting with their friends. "Uncle Henry, can I walk home with Rissy and Clio?" I asked.

He shook his head. "It wouldn't be proper."

I made a face. I didn't know about proper, but it would be fun. Of course, I reminded myself, Uncle Henry and Aunt Laura weren't fun-loving folks. Between the two of them, they had about enough joy and adventurousness to fill a thimble.

I shook my head at Rissy to let her know I couldn't walk home with her. She smiled and shrugged.

Since I didn't know anybody in the churchyard to talk to, I amused myself by kicking a stone around in a circle. I tried to kick it fast enough to keep it moving. I'd gotten pretty good at it when I heard Aunt Laura say, "Hello, Simon and Eliza. How are you folks?"

That must be Mr. and Mrs. Craikey, I thought. I stopped kicking the stone and stared at Simon Craikey to see what a man who owned slave-chasing dogs looked like. I'd figured he might have horns and a tail, like the Devil himself, but he was pretty normal-looking. He was shorter and heavier than Uncle Henry and had a red face, bushy gray sideburns, and a mouth that turned down at the corners. His wife was tall and skinny, all angles in her dark muslin dress. Her face was thin, her nose long, and her eyes pale blue. I couldn't see her hair, because it was hidden under a fancy black bonnet. I hoped for her sake that it was uncommonly nice, because otherwise she was about as pretty as a peeled snake.

My uncle and Mr. Craikey talked about hogs and wheat, and Aunt Laura and Mrs. Craikey exchanged some words on the weather. Then Mrs. Craikey nodded toward me. "Is that her?" she asked Aunt Laura in a hushed voice. "Is that the little gal you've taken in?"

I looked down at the ground, feeling my face turn pink.

"Yes, she's my poor sister's daughter," Aunt Laura replied.

Mrs. Craikey sighed and shook her head. "Well, if she's

kinfolk, I suppose you have to do your Christian duty. Even so, I don't envy you, taking in an orphan."

My head jerked up. "I'm not an orphan! I have a pa!"

Mrs. Craikey gasped.

"Mary Gillian, you apologize at once!" Aunt Laura said sternly.

"But it's true. I'm *not* an orphan! I have a pa, and he loves me and he's going to send for me any day now, as soon as he—"

"*Mary Gillian!*" That was Uncle Henry.

Mr. Craikey chuckled. "I think she needs a hickory switch, Henry."

"I do not!" I cried indignantly.

"Get in the wagon," Uncle Henry ordered me.

As I scuffed toward the wagon, I heard Mrs. Craikey cluck her tongue and say, "Laura, dear, you're surely earning your place in heaven caring for *that* one."

The trip home was very quiet. Sarah and Neddy seemed to know I was in trouble. Sarah gave me worried looks, and Neddy stuck out his tongue and crossed his eyes to make me laugh. I smiled at him the best I could, but I had to try hard not to cry. I wasn't an orphan, and I didn't want to be Aunt Laura's ticket to heaven. I didn't need a hickory switch, either. I needed home and Pa. And I would have them as soon as either he sent for me or the middle of June got here.

I had planned to go out to the woods that afternoon, to start on number two of my list: "Figure out how to get away from here without getting caught." I also wanted to sit on that tree branch over the river again and do some more thinking. But as a punishment for talking back to the Craikeys, I had to read the Bible from dinnertime until suppertime. I didn't even get to read the good parts, like Jonah in the whale's belly or Daniel in the lions' den. I had to read Job.

"It will teach you patience and humility," Uncle Henry said.

So I sat on the pink-and-green-flowered sofa in the parlor and stared at the fat brown Bible's tiny print while Aunt Laura sat at her desk and wrote letters. I didn't read about the afflictions of old Job, though. I looked at the pages and thought about Pa.

Why hadn't my aunt and uncle corrected Mrs. Craikey when she called me an orphan? They knew I had a pa. They might not like him, but they knew I had him. They knew I wasn't an orphan.

What makes you so sure? asked a nasty little voice in my head. It sounded like Mrs. Craikey's. *You haven't heard from your pa in nearly four months. Lots of things can happen to people who go out West, even if they do intend to come back.*

I thought of the three bedraggled men who'd come back to Prairie Flower from the Rockies. One morning last winter, I'd overheard them talking after a church service:

"Remember them two fellas that got drowned in the creek?" one had asked. "Water carried them off—weren't nothin' nobody could do." Another had drawled, "Yeaaah, them floods was awful, all right. But the worst was the fires. They'd tear through a whole camp, kill everybody in it." The third had said, "Fires, nothin'. It was the snakes that was the worst. Kill you before you knew what happened." Then he'd added, "Or maybe it was the landslides that was the worst, or the sicknesses, or the brawlin' and shootin'. Hard to say what was the worst. The whole place, I guess."

So, Gilly Bucket, what makes you so sure you're not an orphan?

"That sniffling won't do you any good," Aunt Laura said. She didn't even look up from her letter writing. "You have to sit there until suppertime, so you may as well stop feeling sorry for yourself."

"I'm not—" I stopped. I'd rather have Aunt Laura think I was pouting than have her know how worried I was about Pa.

I wiped my sleeve across my face, gritted my teeth, and tried to read the verses in front of me. I could certainly feel sorry for Job, losing his fortune and his family. Still, the type was tiny and the words were long, and I kept thinking of how much I missed Pa and how much I hated the Craikeys. After a while I skipped to the end of the story, where Job was richly rewarded for his patience and people wished they hadn't mocked him.

I grinned, thinking of how I'd be rewarded, too. Pa would come riding up to Glencaren on a white horse—no, he'd be in a silver coach pulled by a team of white horses. Rufus Peacock, wearing satin britches and a gold waistcoat, would be driving them. The Craikeys would stand and stare, green with envy. Pa would march up the front steps, bang on the door, and demand that I be returned to him. My aunt and uncle would be seized with fear and sorrow. "You can have her, Mr. Bucket, sir," Uncle Henry would say, "but I'm afraid she's gone blind. It was our own fault. We made her sew and read the Bible too much. If we'd thought you'd really come for her, we'd have treated her better."

Aunt Laura said, "I hardly think Job is a story to chuckle over."

"Yes, ma'am—I mean, no, ma'am."

How, I wondered, had dull, sour old Aunt Laura and Uncle Henry managed to produce gentle Sarah and story-loving Neddy? Maybe the stork had dropped my cousins down the wrong chimney. They were actually the children of a jolly, kind couple somewhere, and the jolly, kind couple had gotten stuck with two tedious, loathsome children who were really Aunt Laura and Uncle Henry's.

I knew the stork didn't really bring babies. I'd seen enough kittens and calves being born to know where they came from, and Granny Pea had even told me how they'd come to be there. Still, the stork idea *would* explain Sarah and Neddy.

I turned back the pages of the Bible and tried again to concentrate on the tiny print. At last my aunt either took pity on me or got tired of hearing me bang my heels against the sofa, and said, "Perhaps you would like to go play Scripture Cards with Neddy."

"No, thank you," I said. Playing Scripture Cards was probably Aunt Laura's idea of a rip-roaring good time.

"Then maybe I can find you another book and you can read in your room."

I liked to read, but I liked lively tales, like *Prairie Flower*, which our town had been named after. Now, *that* was a good book! But knowing Aunt Laura, she'd choose a book about an ornery child, probably one with red hair, who misbehaved and got turned into a toad.

I had an idea. "Could I have some paper and a pen?" I asked. "I want to write a letter to the Cadwalladers to thank them for keeping me. I'll need two sheets of paper, since I have so much to thank them for."

My aunt smiled and got some paper and an envelope out of her desk drawer.

"I'm glad to see you're grateful," she said, handing them to me. "You may sit at my desk and write while I read my *Ladies' Repository* magazine."

I didn't waste much time thanking the Cadwalladers.

After all, they'd never thanked *me* for doing the housework and taking care of the baby. All I wrote to them was:

April 24, 1859

Dear Mister and Missus Cadwallader:

Thank you for keeping me. I got here safe. I hope Baby Bert has stopped hollering. Please give this note to Pa when he gets there in case he never got my letter that says where I am.

Yours truly, I remain, ever grateful,

Mary Gillian Bucket

My *real* letter was to Pa:

April 24, 1859

My dearest dear own Pa,

If you didn't get my last letter and don't know it yet, Granny Pea passed on and I am with Ma's kin now. It is Mr. Henry Hayden's farm in Virginia. Please send for me, Pa! Not an hour goes by that I don't miss you. Sometimes I think I shall never see you again in this world. Oh the sorrow that fills my heart! I truly do not care about the gold, it is you I long for.

Love, love, love,

Your own loving child,

Gilly Bucket

P.S. Tell Rufus his ma went quick and did not suffer.

P.S. again. I send my love to you on the first star each evening. Watch for it and send your love back to me.

P.S. again. You were right about Aunt Laura.

I wanted to tell Pa that if I didn't hear from him by the middle of June, I'd set out to find him. But I knew the Cadwalladers would read my note, even though I wrote PRIVATE FOR PA on the outside when I folded it over.

I sealed the envelope with the letters inside, and left it on the hall table with Aunt Laura's letters.

After dinner I sat on the edge of the back porch to watch for Rissy's and my star. Before it appeared, though, Rissy saw me and came over from the kitchen.

"Clio heard you got in trouble for sassin' Mas' and Miz Craikey in the churchyard," she said, sitting down beside me. "Is it true?"

I nodded. "Mrs. Craikey called me an orphan, like I didn't have a pa to care for me! I told her I wasn't any orphan, and Uncle Henry and Aunt Laura got mad at me for talking back. But what was I supposed to do, act like Pa's dead or abandoning me?"

"Don't you pay no attention to what people say," Rissy replied stoutly. "Just 'cause somebody says somethin' don't make it so. After my daddy left, Mas' Ellicott and them spread the word that he'd been shot and killed."

I looked at her, horrified.

She said, "We knew they was lyin', though, 'cause we'd already overheard them talkin' amongst themselves about how they'd never seen hide nor hair of him. See, every time somebody ran off, the white folks said he'd been shot or eaten by wolves or some such thing. They figured that'd make the rest of us too scared to try it."

Tolliver yelled, "You done with them dishes, new gal?"

"No, sir!" Rissy rolled her eyes. "I gotta go back now. Tolliver's makin' me wash the dishes all over again, 'cause he said I missed a couple of spots."

"I can send your love to your pa," I told her, "but you have to be the one to close your eyes and think on him."

"I can do that while I'm washin' dishes." She sighed and shook her head. "I used to think I'd rather be a house servant than a field hand. But now I ain't so sure. At least when I worked in the field, I got Sundays off."

She went back to her pile of dishes. I stayed outside until our star shone brightly.

"Send my love to Pa," I whispered, "and send Rissy's love to her pa."

Then I closed my eyes and hugged Pa as hard as I could.

I whispered, "I'll try to keep thinking you're alive and I'm not an orphan. But it sure would make it easier if you'd send me even one little short letter."

I'd forgotten about my promise to tell Neddy wildcat stories, but he hadn't.

"Sunday's over, Gilly! You have to tell me about the wildcats now," he said before we'd even gone down to breakfast.

I giggled at his excitement. "Let me at least eat breakfast and do my chores first."

"Okay. But don't forget, you said you'd show me that wildcat money."

When I went up to the attic for the dollar, I lifted Pa's fiddle out of the trunk and stroked it lovingly. It looked lonely and forlorn. I remembered how my feet would start dancing when Pa played "Old Zip Coon," and how "My Old Kentucky Home" would seem to pull the soul right out of me.

Would Pa ever make this fiddle sing again?

I put the fiddle back into the trunk, and picked up my list of things to do before I could set out for the Rockies. I still didn't know how I'd get any food or money.

If I had money, I thought, I could buy provisions along the way. I could take some biscuits and apples to eat on the first day. Then, once I'd gotten to a place where nobody'd know me, I'd find a store. I'd say I was buying things for my ma and pa.

But I didn't have any money and I didn't have anything to sell except the fiddle, the quilt, and the candlesticks that were in this trunk. And my pendant, of course—but I wouldn't part with *it* until I was dead. Besides, I had no way to get to a market to sell things.

"I'll come and find you, Pa," I whispered. "I don't know how I'll do it, but I'll figure out something."

Since Neddy had waited so long to hear about the wildcats, I came up with a really good, bloodcurdling yarn for him.

"Pa and I saved all the people of Prairie Flower from getting eaten," I started out. As I went along, I put in half a dozen wildcats, as well as some babies and elderly folks who were doomed until Pa and I came to the rescue. We wrestled the wildcats bare-handed, twirled them around by the tails, and flung them all over the place. We skinned them and used their pelts to make coats for children in poorhouses.

"And after we killed those wildcats," I finished, "the people had a celebration to honor Pa and me. That's when they gave us the wildcat money. Here it is." I fished it out of my pocket and held it up. "See? It's from the Grand Liberty Bank of East Missouri. That's one of the banks that makes wildcat money. Other banks make bear money and rattlesnake money, to reward people who've killed those things."

"Wow!" Neddy fingered it. "I'll trade you for it. Please, Gilly! You can have anything of mine you want."

I thought quickly. I had planned to give the dollar to him, but if he was volunteering to trade me for it—well, I sure could use some real, honest-to-goodness money for my running away.

"You can't spend this dollar, Neddy," I said, "because it's not any good east of the Mississippi. If you try to spend it here, you'll get thrown into the calaboose."

"What's that?"

"It's a—well, you'd better hope you never find out. But if you want the wildcat money to *have* and not spend, I guess I could sell it to you for some real—I mean, some *eastern*-style money."

"I have a half eagle Papa gave me for my birthday last month! It's worth five dollars. You can have it if you'll give me the wildcat dollar."

My heart thumped with joy, but I pretended to consider his offer reluctantly. "Oh, I suppose that's good enough. But don't ever tell your pa. It might hurt his feelings if he knew you'd traded it."

He promised, and we ran upstairs to exchange money.

I felt a surge of guilt about tricking him. But, I reasoned, the trade had been his idea. He was tickled with his wildcat dollar. Besides, when Pa and I were rich, I'd send him a whole *bag* of half eagles.

I went up to the attic to put my new half eagle into my trunk. Now that I have some money, I thought, I should feel ready to start out. I pictured that map in Uncle Henry's atlas, and tried to imagine walking across the country to the Rocky Mountains. Fifteen hundred miles. Step by step. By myself.

"Courage and determination," I whispered. But it would take a heap of it to last me all the way to Pikes Peak.

5

HAVING RISSY AT UNCLE HENRY'S perked up my life enormously. Sarah and Neddy were my friends, too, but Sarah was busy getting ready for her wedding and Neddy was too young for me to spill out my heart to. Anyway, neither one of them understood about Pa, the way Rissy did. Even though she had to work long hours in the kitchen and I was busy with housecleaning and sewing, I knew we would usually be able to meet in the evenings to send our loves to our pas and talk for a spell. And when we saw each other during the day, we could grin and wave, or roll our eyes behind Aunt Laura's back if she was scolding.

After supper on Tuesday, I helped Rissy clear the dining table. I took the dirty dishes to her at one end of the table. She scraped the leftovers into a bowl, to add to the hogs' food. Then she stacked the dishes in a basket so she could carry them out to the kitchen and wash them.

"I heard Miz Sarah say her daddy was goin' to fetch the mail today," she said. "I don't suppose you got a letter from your pa, did you?"

I shook my head glumly. "If I'd heard from Pa, you wouldn't need to ask. I'd be dancing and shouting for pure joy."

"I know, but I was hopin' just the same." Her sympathetic smile made me feel better.

I hadn't told Rissy about my plan to run away and find Pa. I knew I'd have to tell her soon, but I wasn't ready to talk about it, even to her. I wanted to hug it close to me for a while longer, like a comfortable quilt—a *fragile* quilt that people might poke holes in, even if they meant well.

To our surprise, the next Saturday afternoon, Tolliver let Rissy have a few hours off.

"He said he'd be glad to have me out of his way," she said. "Hmmph! Sayin' I've been in his way, after all the work I've done!"

We played a game with Neddy and Carter, throwing a ball back and forth to each other over the top of Dilsey and Isaac's cabin. Whoever threw the ball had to race around to the other side of the cabin, catch it before it hit the ground, and throw it back. We whooped and hollered and shrieked. Dilsey and little Nancy sat on the doorstep and whooped, too, to encourage us.

After a while, the two boys left with Isaac and Zeke to go fishing in the river. I ran into the house and got one of Neddy's primers and his slate. Rissy and I went deep into the woods, where nobody but birds and wild critters went, and sat down under a tulip poplar to have her first reading lesson.

That girl was as smart as a steel trap! She raced right through the first two lessons, "The cat has a rat," and "The man sat on a hat." Then I added some words, writing the new sentences out on Neddy's slate.

She read slowly, following the words with her index finger. "The bad cat has a sad, mad rat. The fat man sat on a hat. The man ma—may—made the hat flat."

I applauded. "By next week, you'll be reading as well as me."

She grinned shyly. "Can we keep goin', through the next lesson?"

So we went through the third lesson, about a lad who sat, and even the fourth one, which involved not only lads, cats, rats, and hats, but dogs and frogs as well. Rissy caught on quickly to which letter combinations made what sounds.

Finally she gave a long sigh. "Guess it's time to go pluck chickens and scrub taters for dinner."

"Will you teach me a song on the way back?" I asked. "Something you used to sing in the tobacco field, maybe."

Rissy hesitated. "You might not like most of those songs, 'cause they don't speak too kindly about white folks. But I guess there's a few I could teach you."

She thought a minute and sang, "Five can't catch me and ten can't hold me. Ho! Round the corn, Gilly! Round the corn, round the corn, round the corn, Gilly! Ho, ho, ho, round the corn, Gilly!"

I laughed, tickled. "Does it really say my name?"

"No, it's supposed to be Sally," she replied, "but Gilly fits, too. I don't know what it means. It's a funny old song some of the hands back at Mas' Percy's used to sing."

We stopped by her and Clio's cabin and hid the book under her straw pallet so she could study it when Clio was out. She smiled all the way back to the kitchen. As I went up the steps to the back porch, I heard her sweet, clear voice: "Ho, ho, ho, round the corn, Gilly!"

Not everybody appreciated Rissy's singing. During the hymn-singing at church the next morning, Mr. Milkweed-Hair (Neddy said his real name was Hezekiah Boggs) gave her a look that was as sour as green persimmons. No wonder, I thought. When you heard Rissy sing "Amazing Grace," it was easy to believe in heaven, but it was awfully hard to believe in hell.

After the service, I heard Mrs. Craikey tell Aunt Laura,

"You'd better keep a sharp eye on that new house gal of yours. She's being downright uppity, calling attention to herself by singing so loud. Besides that, she's too pretty for her own good. It's the pretty slave gals that cause the trouble, you know."

Mrs. Snakey-Craikey, I thought, looking at her long, skinny body and beady eyes. No wonder she disliked Rissy for being pretty.

"Rissy seems to be quiet and obedient," Aunt Laura replied. "If she causes trouble, I'm sure Clio and Tolliver will let me know."

Mrs. Craikey smiled. "Clio and Tolliver! Now, *those* two are real gems."

"They certainly are," Aunt Laura agreed warmly. "I don't know how I'd get along without them."

I was glad they couldn't see the face I made.

After dinner, I put on my old red-and-blue-plaid dress and ran out to the woods. It was a perfect day to start numbers two and three on my list: "Figure out how to get away from here without getting caught" and "See what grows in these parts to use for food and cures."

I loved this time of year, when nature was full awake but hadn't gotten dry and tuckered out, the way it would later in the summer. There were so many shades of green. The sun shining on the treetops made them the color of the friendly little green snakes we had at home. Farther down, everything was a rich, deep green, and near the ground it was a dark green—the color that cool would be if it was a color, I decided.

On both sides of the narrow woods path, tall grasses and bushes rustled against my skirt. I stopped and studied the plants, to see what I could eat or use for cures when I ran away. Near the creek grew lady's slipper, which was a good sedative. I didn't think I'd need a sedative on my trip West, but I liked looking at the pale yellow, moccasin-shaped blooms. Then I saw jewelweed, which I could plaster on my skin if I got poison ivy. I also found nettles, pokeweed, St. John's wort, mugwort, and sassafras, all of which made good cures.

But you have to have a kettle or pan to boil them in. The voice in my head sounded like Pa's, quiet and reasonable.

"I know," I muttered, "but I haven't figured how to get one."

Some things, such as blackberries and mayapples, wouldn't be edible until July. Nuts and persimmons wouldn't be ready until fall, and by then I'd be in the Rockies with Pa. But there were plenty of dandelions, burdock, wood sorrel, and violets, for salads. And I could always catch fish, rabbits, and squirrels. There were even spicebushes and wild ginger plants to flavor them with.

And how are you going to get these fish and critters? That was Pa's voice again. *You think they'll just take off their skins, jump into the fire, and cook themselves? No, Gilly-girl. You'll*

need a fishing line, traps, boning and scraping knives, and a fry-
ing pan.

How could I possibly get all those things? Or carry them if I had them?

"Courage and determination," I told myself. But you couldn't boil herbs or fry meat in courage and determination.

Monday was washday at Uncle Henry's. I saw old Josie out in the back yard, stirring the clothes as they boiled in an iron pot and then pounding them with a batten to beat the dirt out. But she stirred and beat with such a passion that she got what she called a kink in her backbone, and Rissy had to do the Tuesday ironing.

"Can I take my sewing out to the laundry room so we can work together?" I asked Aunt Laura.

She thought. "All right, but both of you pay attention to your work. I don't want any sloppy stitches or scorch marks."

"Yes, ma'am."

Before leaving the house, I checked the mail. No letters for me. I gave a long sigh. All Pa had to do was scrawl a few words on a scrap of paper: *Gilly, I'm well and want you here.* That was all I needed.

When I got out to the laundry room, Rissy already had the skirt board set up, with the wide end resting on the stone sink and the narrow one resting on the work-table.

"I used to help Mama do the ironin', so it's like old times," she said. She unrolled Sarah's pink dress from the damp cloth it was wrapped in and spread the skirt over the board. "Besides, it's nice to get away from that old Tolliver for a while."

"I just saw him out in the garden," I said.

Rissy snapped the wooden handle onto one of the hot flatirons that sat in a row on the hearth. She tested it on a cloth and then started ironing the dress.

"He saw you and me gazin' on our star the other night," she said as she ironed. "When I got back to the kitchen, he said, 'You tryin' to get familiar with them stars, new gal?' like he thought I was learnin' about the sky so I'd know how to run North. I smiled at him real sweet and said, 'Why, no, sir, I just like to look at all them stars and think on what beauteous things the Lord hath made.' "

We both giggled.

She lowered her voice. "Dilsey says Tolliver told Mas' Hayden and Mas' Craikey where to hunt for some slaves that ran off last month."

I gasped. "Patsy and the others?"

She nodded. "Isaac, Dilsey's husband, overheard Mas' Craikey talkin' to him. Mas' Craikey said if Tolliver helped them find the runaways, he'd get a big reward he could

84

keep for himself. He might have figured he could use it to buy his freedom someday."

"You mean he was willing to send those other people back into slavery so he could maybe go free someday?"

Rissy nodded. "Not only that, but he knew if Mas' Craikey found his field hands, he'd whup them nearly to death. Everybody in the quarters says Mas' Craikey's the meanest man around."

"I know. He has slave-chasing dogs, too," I said. Then I remembered something. "Rissy, have you ever heard of a train that runs underground?"

"Yes'm, my daddy took that train!" she said excitedly. "He said he was gonna ride it all the way to Canada."

"Does it really run underground?"

She shrugged. "I asked Daddy that, and he said he didn't know. He said he reckoned it didn't matter as long as it got him away from Mas' Ellicott, that overseer."

"Hmm." I thought. "Have you ever heard of somebody called the Spirit? He helps black folks escape, but nobody knows who he is or how he works."

"The Spirit." Rissy mused on it. "No, but I'll see what I can find out."

Clio came to the door. "Miz Gilly, your aunt be askin' for you."

"Okay," I said. Impulsively, I asked, "Clio, do you know anything about an underground railroad or somebody called the Spirit?"

She caught her breath. "Gal, where'd you hear about them things? Was it from one of the black folks?"

"No, it was from Uncle Henry."

"You better not be talkin' about them anymore," she said. "Somebody'll think one of us be plannin' to light out of here."

The only person I knew who was planning to light out of there was me, but I couldn't say that. "Tell Aunt Laura I'll be right there," I told Clio.

"Yes'm. She says she got a heap more mendin' for you to do if you finish what you got there."

After Clio had left, Rissy took the pink dress off the skirt board and unrolled Aunt Laura's brown shirtwaist. She said, "Can you come stay with me in the kitchen until late Saturday night? I gotta be there by myself. I ain't hankerin' to be alone with that ghost upstairs—not even if I'm able to find a ghost charm by then."

"Okay," I replied. "Bring the primer and we'll read. But why will you be alone? Where are Tolliver and Clio going?"

"There's gonna be a dance down at the quarters." Rissy lowered her voice. "Clio's goin'. I think she's got a beau!"

"Clio?"

Rissy giggled. "Hard to believe, ain't it? But a couple of nights ago, I woke up and saw her slip out the cabin door. I figured she was goin' to the necessary house, but then I woke up a long time later and she wasn't back yet. Only reason I can think of is she was meetin' a beau—maybe somebody from Mas' Craikey's. Anyways, don't tell nobody."

I promised, but I was tickled at the idea of prim-and-proper Clio running off in the night to meet a beau.

"Is Tolliver going to the dance, too?" I asked.

"Him?" Rissy snorted. "He'd break like a dry old tree branch if he had to unbend himself enough to dance! Clio says he turns up his nose at the goin's-on down at the cabins, and goes to bed early on Saturday nights."

"I bet everybody's glad he doesn't come," I said, trying to imagine having a good time with Tolliver watching. I got up and stretched. "I'd better go get the rest of Aunt Laura's mending. If I don't do it now, it'll be waiting for me tomorrow."

But the next day I got a rest from sewing.

"Mary Gillian and Neddy, I need you to drip the lye for soap-making," Aunt Laura said at dinner.

Sarah quickly said, "I should help, too, Mama. After all, most of the soap's for David's and my new home."

"Nonsense!" Aunt Laura said. "I won't have you going to your wedding with a red face and chapped hands."

Nobody was worried about Neddy or me having a red face and chapped hands. Our feet didn't seem to be of much importance, either—we nearly walked them off that afternoon, carrying pail after pail of water to pour into the barrel of fireplace ashes that had collected all winter.

"The water and ashes mix together to make lye," I explained to my cousin.

"I don't care," he said grouchily. "My feet hurt."

"Let's pretend we're walking out West to find—to find gold," I told him. I'd almost said *to find Pa*.

As we walked, we pointed out the imaginary rivers and mountains we were passing, and wondered how close we must be to the gold mines by now. At first it was fun, but then I thought about how today was May fourth and I still hadn't heard from Pa. I'd been *sure* I'd hear from him yesterday and had run to meet Uncle Henry when he came home with the mail. But I'd looked through the pile of mail twice, and there hadn't been a letter for me.

I felt the familiar black, hot, scared feeling overtake me. How could Pa be alive and not have written to me for this long?

"I'm kind of tired," I told Neddy. "Let's pretend we've already found our gold."

It was suppertime before we had enough lye. I was afraid we'd have to stay out there all night finishing up, but Aunt Laura said, "We'll do the rest tomorrow."

What she meant by "the rest" was the actual soap-making itself. Clio and I melted down a great hunk of fat in a big cast-iron pot, and Aunt Laura stirred in the lye.

Once the mixture had started to boil, Aunt Laura

added some quicklime, and then she and Clio and I took turns stirring it. While I was stirring, the froth settled and large white bubbles started to pop. "It's almost ready!" I called to my aunt.

When it had gotten thick and ropy, we carried most of it down to the cellar in pails and poured it into a barrel to cool. "Let the rest of it stay in the kettle," Aunt Laura directed, throwing some more salt into the kettle. "We'll use it to make cakes of Sarah's complexion soap."

Clio left to help Tolliver in the kitchen, and my aunt and I took turns stirring the thick soap mixture. Finally she said all the excess water had been "salted out."

"What do we do now?" I asked. I'd never made hard soap before. Granny Pea and I had made barrels of soft soap and used it for everything.

"We'll let it cool until tomorrow," she told me. "Then we'll boil it again with some turpentine and more salt, and pour it into molds."

So Friday found us still making soap. I hopped up and down impatiently while Clio took her turn stirring and Aunt Laura prepared the molds.

"Clio," my aunt said, "go up to the herb room and get the jar of dried lavender. We'll spread it on some muslin and set the cakes of soap on it so they'll absorb the scent while they're hardening." She took a key off the jangling ring at her waist and handed it to Clio. "The lavender is on a shelf in the storeroom."

"I'll get it," I offered eagerly.

"Clio will get it," Aunt Laura said firmly. "You take over the stirring."

"But why can't I get it? I'm not busy. Besides, I want to see your herb room."

"No, Mary Gillian, I do *not* want you going up there. Is that clear?"

"But— Yes, ma'am." I took the stirring paddle from Clio. I didn't want to spend another afternoon reading Job.

"Why doesn't she want me to go up to her precious herb room?" I grumbled to Rissy when I went out to the kitchen Saturday night. "After all, I was Granny Pea's apprentice. I know how to act in an herb room. I wouldn't knock anything over or mix up her herbs. I bet she's scared I'll steal those secret recipes she's so proud of."

Rissy looked up from the copper pot she was scrubbing. "I asked old Josie about that ghost she thinks lives up there. She said she heard it when she was workin' in the laundry room one night. She said the floorboards creaked, like somebody was walkin' around, then it commenced to wailin' like a lost soul. She said it was the saddest, most pitiful wailin' she ever heard, even worse than you'd hear at a buryin'."

"What did she do?"

"She dropped the pan of water she was carryin' and ran outta here, a-shriekin' and a-hollerin'. She won't come back after dark no more. Clio says Josie's old and hearin' things, but I went on and got me that ghost charm, anyway. See?"

From under the bodice of her dress she pulled out a little furry thing that hung around her neck on a leather thong. "It's a rabbit's foot Jupiter gave me. He said it's from a rabbit that was caught by a cross-eyed man in a graveyard at midnight. That's the most powerful kind."

"It's nice," I said, stroking the soft fur. "But Granny Pea didn't believe in ghosts. She said that when you think there's a ghost, it's always something else and you have to find out what it is."

Rissy looked at me. "You mean you're goin' upstairs to find out what Josie's ghost is?"

"No, I'm going upstairs to see Aunt Laura's herb room. But if there's a ghost up there, I guess I'll see it, too."

"You goin' tonight? In the dark?"

"Well—no. I'll wait until tomorrow morning, while everybody's at church. I'll say I feel puny and want to stay home. That way I can be sure Aunt Laura and Tolliver won't come up and find me."

"You want to borrow my rabbit's foot?"

"No, thanks. I'm not scared," I said—even though I was, a little.

That evening we didn't hear anything overhead except a mouse skittering and a few normal night creaks. If there *was* a ghost living in the herb room and it could hear us, it got treated to a story about a fox chasing a hen, and it learned how to spell "Rissy," "Gilly," "Mama," "Daddy," and "Canada."

When I told Aunt Laura I didn't feel like going to church, she said, "I suppose I'd better stay home and look after you."

"You don't have to," I said quickly.

To my relief, Sarah said, "I'll stay with her. I feel a little poorly myself."

Because I said I didn't feel well, I was given only toast for breakfast and had to swallow a spoonful of castor oil. Sarah didn't get any castor oil. I asked Neddy why, and he said that after you turned thirteen, it didn't help anymore.

When everybody else had left for church, I got dressed and languished on the sofa for a while, trying to look pale. Sarah leafed through some *Godey's Lady's Book* journals, then went upstairs to take a nap. I ran out to the kitchen, ate the leftover pancakes and a couple of cold sausages, and hurried upstairs.

As I climbed the winding stone steps, I got a creepy feeling that made me wish I'd borrowed Rissy's rabbit's foot, after all. But once upstairs, I couldn't imagine a ghost living in that big, dry, airy herb room. What a joy it must be to work here, I thought. Granny Pea would have loved it.

The room was purposeful and uncluttered. Its pine floor was swept perfectly clean. Overhead were wooden rafters where bunches of rosemary, thyme, betony, and wormwood hung. Several large baskets sat waiting to be filled. Plenty of light came in from the windows, but the white curtain kept direct sunbeams from hitting the herbs and sucking out their fragrant oils.

I walked over to look closely at the white curtain. I lifted up the corner, the way I'd seen it lifted my first night here, and dropped it again. I frowned. There wasn't anything that could have done that except somebody's hand. But I still didn't think the herb room had a ghost living in it. It was as far from being a spooky, haunted kind of place as I could imagine.

I continued my walk around the room. A worktable against one wall held a small set of scales, a heavy wooden cutting board, a mortar and pestle for pounding herbs into powders, and a small wooden box. A longer, completely bare table stood across the room. Along the far wall was an apothecary's chest. Through its glass doors I could see labeled tins and dark jars of herbs. The only other pieces of furniture were several straight cane-bottom chairs. Aunt Laura's herb room was perfectly equipped and had plenty of space for storing, drying, and stripping herbs and processing them into remedies.

There was a small, square room built into a back corner. I tried to open the door, but the knob wouldn't turn. I guessed it was the storage room where Aunt Laura kept her valuable prepared remedies and store-bought herbs. Sarah had said it was always kept locked.

Seeing no sign of a ghost, I sat down at the worktable and reached for the wooden box. Did it hold the secret recipes Aunt Laura bragged about?

I opened the box and found it filled with neatly printed recipes. Ha, I thought, looking at the first two. These were the same old recipes for cough syrups that everybody knew: one used wild cherry bark, mullein leaves, horehound, and sugar, and the other used persimmon bark, sage, alum, and molasses. There was nothing secret about *them*! Besides, Granny Pea had said that sumac berries boiled in water and honey worked better than either of those.

The next few recipes were for rheumatism cures: a salve of strong mullein tea mixed with lard; a poultice of pokeroot, and a poultice of lavender, rosemary, and brandy. Again, there was nothing secret or special about those.

I read all of Aunt Laura's herb recipes. Not even one was unusual.

Mixed in with the recipes was a piece of paper, folded over. I unfolded it and found that it was not a recipe but a note in spidery brown writing.

April 9, 1859

Dear Mrs. Hayden:

I am expecting the order of herbs from my supplier in Richmond any day now. As promised, I shall send you one large order of lady's slipper and one very small order of St. John's wort. If they are strong enough, mix both with four cups of water and steep for thirty minutes.

I remain, at your service,

Dr. Anselm Granger

Didn't Dr. Granger and Aunt Laura know that lady's slipper and St. John's wort grew in the woods around here? I'd seen them myself, just last Sunday!

Maybe they figured that fancy store-bought herbs worked better than woods-grown ones. But I remembered the conversation Dr. Granger and I had had the night he brought me home from the train station. We'd been talking about herbs, and I'd told him what Granny Pea had always said: wild herbs had to be strong in order to survive, and they put that quality into the person who partook of them. Dr. Granger had nodded and said, "Your Granny Pea was exactly right. We're lucky that so many wild herbs grow in the woods around here." Why had he said that if he'd just sent Aunt Laura a shipment of store-bought herbs? Besides, what did he mean by "mix both with four cups of water"? He didn't even say how *much* of them to mix with the water!

I put everything back where I'd found it, closed the recipe box, and made sure I hadn't left any signs of my being there. As I returned to the house, I pondered what I'd seen: the white curtain that had moved for no reason, the not-so-secret recipes Aunt Laura guarded, and the note from Dr. Granger that didn't make any sense.

Even though I didn't believe Aunt Laura's herb room was haunted, I knew there was something funny going on up there.

6

AFTER DINNER, I had to convince Aunt Laura that I had recovered enough to go out. "The castor oil must have made me well," I told her.

"Or maybe *some*body just didn't want to go to church," she replied. "I think perhaps you should stay inside and rest this afternoon."

"But I feel fine," I insisted, "and Rissy doesn't get much time off. If we don't play together today, we might not be able to for *weeks*."

At last my aunt relented. "But no horsing around or tree climbing. Find some quiet activity."

"Yes, ma'am." Reading was about as quiet an activity as you could do.

I walked sedately to the back door. Then, outside

where my aunt could no longer see me, I ran to the quarters as fast as a bolt of greased lightning.

"I'm sure glad to see you, Gilly," Rissy said. "I had a worry worm all mornin'."

"A worry worm?"

She explained, "Whenever my mama felt troubled, she'd say, 'I got a worry worm gnawin' at my innards.' An' I surely had one thinkin' of you up there in that place where the ghost lives."

"I didn't see any ghost," I assured her, "and I don't think there is one."

She didn't look convinced. "Maybe it only comes out at night. That's what ghosts do, isn't it? Sleep all day and roam around wailin' all night?"

"Maybe," I agreed. "But that herb room doesn't look like a place a ghost would live. I *did* find some other odd things, though."

I told her about Dr. Granger's strange note and Aunt Laura's recipes.

"I didn't see anything that could have made that curtain move, either," I finished.

Rissy said, "I don't care what your Granny Pea said, I'm gonna keep wearin' my rabbit's foot till we puzzle out what's goin' on up there. Leastways, it'll be a long time before I have to work in that kitchen by myself at night again. The next party's gonna be the night before Miz Sarah's weddin', and Clio says we all get to go to that.

Mas' Hayden's even gonna give us a hog to barbecue! Mas' Craikey's people are invited, too."

She made a face. "That old Mas' Craikey was lookin' me over this mornin', while I was waitin' for the others in the churchyard. Ugh! He looked at me like he was thinkin' about what I look like under my dress." She lowered her voice. "I hear he *uses* his gals, if you know what I mean. If they don't let him have his way with them, he whups them."

I gasped. "I heard Uncle Henry say that Mr. Craikey wanted you. Thank goodness, Uncle Henry had already"—I couldn't bring myself to say *bought you*—"had already spoken for you himself."

"I sure am lucky about that." Rissy shuddered. "I'd rather swallow a bullfrog whole than have to work for Mas' Craikey."

We waved to Neddy and Carter, who were playing marbles on the ground outside the cabins, and walked out into the woods. We sat under the same tree as before.

Rissy read an exercise about a boy named Tom who was kind to a blind man and one about a cat wanting to rob a bird's nest. She read slowly and followed the words with her finger, but she didn't stumble or hesitate very often. After she'd learned all the words in the exercises, I taught her to spell "food," "water," and "Hayden." We scratched them in the dirt with the sharp ends of twigs.

"Teach me a long, fancy word to spell!" she said.

I taught her "Mississippi," which she found a source of wonderment.

"It's like 'Rissy,' but it keeps on goin'," she said.

We got the giggles, making all those s's in the dirt.

Rissy commented, "I've heard the word 'Mississippi,' but I didn't know it would be fun to spell. It's the name of a place down South. Black folks say if you get sold to a plantation down there, you'll be pickin' cotton in the hot sun till you drop dead."

"It's also the name of a big, wide, muddy river," I told her. "I crossed it on the way here. It's lots wider than the Potomac! I don't know how I'm going to get across it when I go out West to look for Pa."

Rissy's forehead wrinkled with puzzlement. "When you what?"

I'd forgotten that Rissy didn't know I was planning to run away. Quietly I said, "I was going to tell you, honest."

Rissy gasped. "You're goin' out West to look for your *pa*? Are you foolin' me?"

"No." I couldn't look at her. I concentrated on rubbing out our words with my writing twig so nobody'd see them. "I'm going to leave in the middle of June, unless Pa sends for me first."

I knew that if I lived to be a hundred and ten, I'd remember that moment: the green canopy of leaves above us, the rustling of the water and the cheerily-cheerily-cheerily of a robin, the little breeze that cooled my forehead, and the hurt and sorrow in Rissy's face as she realized how soon I'd be leaving.

I saw her swallow a lump in her throat.

"I know how it is when you want to go find your daddy," she said slowly. "I don't blame you a bit. It's just that—well, you bein' my first friend and all—I hadn't figured on you goin' away anytime soon."

"I know," I said. "You're my first friend, too, and I don't want to leave you, either. But somebody's got to find Pa, and I don't hear anybody else volunteering."

We sat there for a minute, each thinking our own thoughts. Suddenly I had an idea that was so grand I couldn't believe it hadn't occurred to me before. "Rissy, you can go with me!" I whispered. "You'd be safe with me. I can make up a story to tell people about how you belong to my family and we're traveling together. Oh, please, say yes!"

She shook her head. "No, Gilly, I can't go with you. I gotta stay here in case my daddy comes lookin' for me. See, he'd most likely go to Mas' Percy's, thinkin' I'd still be there. If I stay here, somebody might be able to tell him where I am. But if I was to leave and go off to those mountains you talk about, he'd never find me. Anyways, I got it pretty good here at Mas' Hayden's, and I don't want to take a chance on gettin' caught runnin' away." She gave me a weak grin. "I might get sold to the *state* of Mississippi."

"I suppose you're right," I said, "but the trip sure would be nicer with you along."

We were both quiet and thoughtful for a few minutes.

Finally Rissy said, "I guess we've always known we'd have to leave each other if our daddies sent for us, but I just hadn't thought about one of us leavin' and one bein' left behind. Seems like everybody keeps leavin' me— Daddy, then Mama, now you. And what makes it harder is, I don't even rightly know where you're goin', not you and Daddy anyway. At least with Mama, I can picture her soul goin' straight up through the clouds to heaven. But Canada and Pikes Peak—I don't know how far off they are, or how you go about gettin' there. They're just names to me. That makes them seem awful far away, even farther away than heaven is."

I said, "Come into the library tomorrow morning, and I'll show you the map in Uncle Henry's atlas. I'll show you where Pikes Peak is, and how I plan to get there. That way, after I leave, you can think about me walking through those places."

Rissy's eyes gleamed, but she said, "If I got caught lookin' at a map, I'd get whupped for sure."

"You won't get caught," I said. "Just tell Clio you'll dust and sweep in the library after you do the breakfast dishes. I'll watch for you. You can pretend to be dusting, and sort of look slanty-eyed at the map in case anybody comes in."

"Will you show me Canada, too? So I'll know where my daddy is?"

"Yes, I will. You can even find it yourself, since you know how to spell it."

"Okay," she agreed. "I'll be in there after breakfast."

I'd never seen anybody as excited as Rissy was when she looked at that map.

"See, here's us, in northern Virginia," I told Rissy, pointing. "Out here is Missouri, where I'm from. And way, way out here is Pikes Peak, where my pa is."

"That surely is a long way!"

"I know. I measured with my finger," I said. "It's fifteen hundred miles."

"And you're gonna *walk* that far?"

"I will to find Pa," I replied. "Now see if you can find Canada on the map."

Rissy's brow wrinkled in concentration as she looked closely at the words. Then she jabbed her finger on the word "Canada," and beamed.

"There it is—Canada! C-A-N-A-D-A. I found it, all by myself! My, it's a big place. What part do you suppose my daddy—"

The library door swung open. We both whirled around. My heart nearly jumped out of my chest.

It was Sarah. "Gilly, are you— What are you girls doing?"

"I was just dustin', Miz Sarah!" Rissy cried quickly.

"You were not dusting, you were looking at a book." Sarah made a scooting motion with her hands. "Go dust the parlor. Run along now. Gilly and I have to talk."

Rissy darted out the door. To my astonishment, Sarah looked stern. Her brown eyes were hard, the way Aunt Laura's often were.

"Gilly, did Rissy ask you to show her that map?"

"Why, no! I was looking to see where—where the Rockies are, so I'd know where Pa is. Rissy came in to dust, and I wanted to show her where I'm from and where Virginia is and where my pa is."

Somehow I knew I'd better not mention Canada.

"Oh, Gilly." Sarah sighed. "Showing slaves how to read a map is the very worst thing you can do. People could say you were helping Rissy get ready to run away. Not only her, but all the slaves she knows and could pass the information to."

I looked down at my feet and didn't answer.

"I suppose you didn't know better," Sarah said, "so I won't tell Mama or Papa. But don't show Rissy any more maps or books, hear? Besides, you shouldn't be in Papa's library. He's very particular about his books."

"Oh, I wouldn't hurt them," I assured her, glad to change the subject. I added proudly, "We had books at home, too. We had a Bible, an almanac, and two books of Ma's: *Pilgrim's Progress* and *Prairie Flower*." I looked at the rows of books that lined Uncle Henry's library wall. "Your pa must sure love to read."

"Well, Papa doesn't actually read very much," Sarah said. "But he wants his books kept nice. He's really proud of them. He has leather-bound collections of the classics that he sent to Boston for, and some volumes of poetry that were printed in France and England. He doesn't like them to be opened. He says it creases their spines."

"But you can't read them if you don't open them!"

Sarah laughed. "Like I said, Papa's not much of a scholar. The only books he ever reads are books on farming. I don't read much, either, I'm afraid—I did all the reading I ever want to in school. Mama doesn't have time to read, and Neddy would rather play."

I thought it was sad that all those books were sitting there unread.

"Now come along," Sarah said. "Mama wants you in the herb garden."

"She does? In the *herb* garden?"

"Yes. Tolliver's rheumatism has flared up, and he can't bend his knees to do the weeding. Mama said she wants it done today in case it starts raining again, but she and I have been invited to tea this afternoon with an old friend of Mama's, Emma Bussy, who's here visiting her kinfolk."

I remembered that name. "She's the lady Aunt Laura got a letter from—her friend from when they were girls. Do you think she knew my ma?"

"She must have, since your ma was Mama's sister," Sarah replied. "She'll be at my wedding, and you can ask her then."

When we got into the hall, I said, "Tell Aunt Laura I'll be out in a minute. I need to see Rissy first, to—to tell her what you said."

Rissy was dusting Aunt Laura's desk. Her back was stiff and she was staring intently at her duster, as if she was trying not to cry. She jumped and caught her breath when she heard me come in.

"Was Miz Sarah mad?" she whispered.

"Yes, but at me, not you," I whispered back. "She was nice, though. She said I shouldn't show you maps or books, but she isn't going to tell anybody."

Rissy sighed with relief. "I'm glad of that, 'cause I can't stop learnin' things now. Besides, even if we did get caught, I'm glad I saw where you're goin' and where my daddy is."

"We'll have to be more careful from now on," I told her. "We'll do all our reading away from the house."

When I got to the herb garden, Aunt Laura said, "I was beginning to think you weren't coming. I need you to do some weeding while Tolliver's laid up with his rheumatism."

"Granny Pea always said the best rheumatism cure is liniment from the oil of a bitternut hickory tree," I said eagerly. "I can tell you how to make it if you want."

"No, Mary Gillian, I have my own recipes for rheuma-tism remedies."

"Yes, ma'am." I'd seen her recipes, and they were good ones. But they must not be helping Tolliver any, if he had to stop working because of his knees. So why wouldn't she at least listen to mine?

"Start here in the coltsfoot patch and work your way around," Aunt Laura was saying. "You *do* know how to tell a weed from a garden herb, don't you?"

"Yes, ma'am."

She looked dubious, but she said, "Well, all right. But remember that coltsfoot flowers look a lot like dandelions. Don't pull up anything you're not sure of."

She nodded a curt goodbye and walked up to the house. I stuck out my tongue at her back. Acting as if I didn't know how to weed an herb garden!

Pretty soon I saw Jupiter bring the horse and buggy around to the front door. Sarah and Aunt Laura, dressed in pale, summery dresses, got in and were driven off down the road. Not long afterward, I saw Uncle Henry and Neddy walking toward the fields.

It was too nice a day to stay mad for long, even at Aunt Laura. The sun shone with a gentle warmth, and a few clouds, white and fluffy as lambs, played across the sky.

I weeded for a long time. The weeds that would make good eating, like dandelions, wild onions, and shamrocks,

I put in a pile to take down to Jupiter and Josie so they could have a nice salad with their supper. When I sat back to rest, I nibbled some shamrock leaves myself. Their lemony flavor reminded me of Granny Pea's beaver stew, which she'd always flavored with shamrock.

I heard a faint clip-clop and saw a little cloud of dust rising from the main road. It was too early for Aunt Laura and Sarah to be coming home, but nobody'd said anything about expecting company. My heart leaped like a deer. Maybe it was Pa!

I scrambled to my feet and shaded my eyes to look. A horse-drawn buggy was entering the front drive. The horse, a bright chestnut with a blaze and white stockings, looked familiar. The man who got out of the buggy looked familiar, too, but it wasn't Pa. It was Dr. Granger.

I waved and yelled, "Dr. Granger, over here!"

He waved back. His footsteps rustled in the grass as he came over to me.

"Afternoon, miss," he said, tipping his hat. "Gilly, isn't it?"

"Yes, sir." I didn't give him my hand, since it was covered with soil.

"I see you're taking good care of your aunt's herbs. Is she or Tolliver around?"

I shook my head. "Aunt Laura and Sarah are making a social call. Tolliver is resting his knees."

"So you're in charge, then! Well, I'll leave your aunt a note up in her herb room."

I said eagerly, "If you need an herb or a remedy, I can help you."

"I'm sure you can," he replied pleasantly, "but I have a patient waiting and can't stay. I'll just leave your aunt Laura a note."

"I can tell her something if you like," I offered. "I wouldn't forget."

"No, no, I don't want to inconvenience you," he said, smiling at me. "I'll leave my calling card on the table in the hallway, and she'll know to look for my note in the herb room. We often stay in touch that way."

He tipped his hat once more. "Nice to see you again, Gilly. Thanks for your help."

He went into the kitchen and, I supposed, up to the herb room. After a few minutes, I saw him walk back to the house and open the front door. He was inside long enough to leave his card, then came out, waved to me, and drove off.

I returned his wave, but my feelings were hurt. Why hadn't he let me help him? That night he'd brought me here, we'd talked about herbs and he'd seemed impressed by all I knew. Maybe he was only being polite, and didn't really think a young girl like me could make remedies. Or maybe Aunt Laura had told him not to let me near her

herb room. Why, she might have told him all *sorts* of un-
kind things about me!

As soon as the doctor was out of sight, I went through
the kitchen and up the stone steps to the herb room. I
wanted to see whether the note he'd left was as odd as the
one I'd found in the recipe box.

His note, written in the same brown spidery writing as
the first one, was lying on Aunt Laura's herb-preparation
table.

May 9, 1859

Dear Mrs. Hayden:

*I have received the large packet of motherwort from
my supplier, and will have it delivered to you as we
arranged. It appears to be healthy and undamaged.
Note that for its preparation you must use six parts
water to one part herb.*

I remain, at your service,

Dr. Anselm Granger

Six parts water to one part herb? That wasn't how you
made motherwort tea! You used a spoonful or two of
motherwort for each cup of water. I knew, because I'd
helped Granny Pea prepare motherwort tea lots of times,
for women who were in childbirth or having trouble with

their monthly courses. It was good for nervous ailments, too, especially if you mixed in some hawthorn berries and chamomile.

Ha! I thought. No wonder Aunt Laura and Dr. Granger didn't want me to help them make their remedies. It wasn't because they didn't trust me, it was because they didn't want me to find out how ignorant they were.

7

ONCE AUNT LAURA was sure Rissy was capable
of helping Clio with the housework, she let me churn
butter.

"You'll still need to help Clio on mornings when Tolliver needs Rissy in the kitchen," she said. "But when he
doesn't, Rissy can help Clio and I'll find other chores for
you: dairy work, weeding the gardens, and so on."

"Yes, ma'am!" I said eagerly. Those things would be
lots more fun than airing the bedding and dusting the
knickknacks with prim, silent Clio every day.

It was cool and pleasant in the stone dairy. Aunt Laura
brought me a pail of milk and a special long-handled cup
to use in skimming the cream off the top of it. As I
skimmed, I poured each cup of cream I got into the tall

wooden butter churn. Then I put in the churn's dasher so that its flat paddles were down in the cream and its broomstick-like handle stuck up from the top of the churn. I fastened on the churn's lid, fitting it down so that the dasher handle came through the hole in the middle.

After that, I worked the dasher up and down as fast as I could for half an hour or so, to agitate the cream until the butter lumps separated from the liquid. I sang the butter-churning chant Granny Pea had taught me, "Come, Butter, Come!" as I worked the dasher up and down.

"Lordy, Mary Gillian, you'll sour the butter with all that caterwauling," Aunt Laura said, coming into the dairy. She chuckled a little, though, so I didn't feel bad. I knew my voice wasn't anything to brag on. "Here's a bowl for the butter and a jar to put the buttermilk in. Has the butter gathered?"

I nodded. "It's starting to. The cream feels thick, and I can hear lumps splashing around." Because it was Tuesday, I asked, "Has Uncle Henry gotten home with the mail?"

"Not yet, but he should be here soon." She hesitated, as if she was going to add something else.

"I'll let you know when the butter's through gathering," I said quickly, and started working the dasher again. If Aunt Laura had a mind to say something about Pa's not writing, I didn't want to hear it.

My aunt left, taking the pail of milk back to the icehouse. I sang a few more rounds of "Come, Butter,

Come!" At last I could tell that the butter had gathered into all the lumps it was going to. I lifted them out with the dasher paddles and scraped them off into the bowl, then poured the leftover cream, which was now buttermilk, from the churn into the glass jar. With my hands, I pressed the butter lumps together to make a big ball. I'd always liked feeling butter ooze through my fingers. Forming butter reminded me of making mud pies, but it was better because I could lick my hands when I was done.

I rinsed the butter ball with cool water, and kneaded some salt into it so it would keep longer. Then I licked the butter off my fingers and wiped them on the grass outside.

As I took the finished butter and the jar of buttermilk to the icehouse, I saw Jupiter drive the buggy up and let Uncle Henry off at the front door. He had the mail with him!

Quickly I took the churn and dasher out to the well, washed them, wiped my hands on my dress, and ran to the house. I had sneezed three times in a row last night, which meant I was *sure* to get a letter!

The table in the hallway held a stack of mail. I flipped through the envelopes quickly, my hands trembling with excitement. But it was the same as always: letters for Miss Sarah Hayden, letters for Mrs. Laura Hayden, bills for Mr. Henry Hayden, nothing for Miss Gilly Bucket.

A hot tear rolled down my face.

"Gilly?"

Sarah came out of the parlor and put an arm around me.

"Gilly? Are you all right? What's wrong?"

"I keep waiting for a letter from Pa, and I never get one." A tear spilled out of my other eye, and I brushed it away with the back of my hand.

"Oh, dear." Sarah sighed. "Let's go sit down."

She helped me into the parlor. We sat on the sofa, and she patted my back while I let the tears flow.

"Do you want me to go get Mama?" she asked anxiously.

"No!"

"Very well, but try to stop crying. Here, take this." She gave me a tiny lace handkerchief that wouldn't have sopped up a bird sneeze. I thanked her and wiped my face the best I could.

"You said you're waiting for a letter from your pa?"

I nodded bleakly. "I look every Tuesday, but there never is one."

Sarah considered. "Well, at least there isn't any *bad* news. If something bad had happened to him, wouldn't somebody have written you?"

"Not if it happened where nobody saw." I gave a small sob. "He might have gotten killed when he was off by himself."

"But didn't you say he had a friend with him?"

"Rufus Peacock. But maybe he got killed, too. Or

maybe—" I couldn't bring myself to say the words: maybe Pa had forgotten me. I pressed my lips together hard to keep from sobbing again.

"Oh, Gilly!" Sarah patted me on the back some more. "I'll bet there's a good reason why you haven't heard from him. As a matter of fact, Papa's always complaining about the mail service here. So maybe your pa wrote and the letter got lost or—or destroyed in a train wreck or something."

"Do you really think so?"

"I think it's possible, and that you shouldn't give up hope. Now, are you all right? Would you like me to have Clio bring you some cookies?"

"No, I'm okay."

Sarah smiled. "I'll tell you what. We still haven't gotten you anything to wear for my wedding. Why don't we go up to the attic and look at dresses? We have time before dinner."

"Okay." There was still a dull ache inside me, but I was cried out. And Sarah could be right—if Uncle Henry thought the mail service was bad, maybe a letter from Pa *had* gotten lost.

"Thanks, Sarah," I said, and we hugged each other.

I followed her upstairs and then up the narrow steps to the attic.

"My outgrown party dresses are in here," she said,

nodding at a trunk in the corner. She knelt down and raised the lid. "Let's see if we can find something you like."

"You must have gone to a lot of parties," I said. I couldn't imagine one person needing so many fancy dresses.

But out of all those dresses, there didn't seem to be one that suited me. Even though I rather fancied myself in fluted frills and pearly loops, Sarah thought I'd look better in something simple. She tossed aside several dresses I liked, because she said they were too flouncy and ruffly. Also, she said, I shouldn't wear the red, purple, or yellow dresses because of my hair color.

"Why not?" I asked. "My hair's the color of a fox. And I'll bet a fox would look okay if it was sitting by clumps of violets and yellow primroses and had a redbird perched on its back."

Sarah laughed so hard that she had to brush away tears from *her* eyes.

"Oh, Gilly, I can't wait for David to meet you," she said. "He's coming for dinner a week from Sunday."

"I'm eager to meet him," I told her. I figured there was a good chance I'd like him, since I liked Sarah and since he was against slavery.

When we were nearly at the bottom of the clothes trunk, I spied a bit of blue.

"What's this?" I asked, and pulled it out. It was a simple muslin dress the color of the early morning sky. It had a high-necked shirred bodice and a plain gathered skirt.

"Oh, that old thing!" Sarah waved a hand. "It's years out of style."

I held it up to myself. "I like it."

Sarah cocked her head. "Hmm, it is a nice color for you."

"It matches my pendant!" I lifted my forget-me-not out from under my calico dress and hung it over the muslin one.

"You're right, it does," Sarah murmured. She nodded. "Go on down to our room and try it on while I pack up these other things. I hope you don't mind if I do the alterations myself instead of having Miss Jenny, our dressmaker, do them. Papa had a fit when he saw the bill I'd run up. I don't dare add anything else."

"I don't mind," I told her. The dress would still be the prettiest I'd ever had.

After dinner, Sarah and I went up to our room, and I stood on a stool and turned slowly around while she marked the hem. Then I jumped down and held out my arms so she could pin tucks in the bodice.

"Sarah," I said slowly. "Yesterday, when you told me I shouldn't have shown Rissy that map, I was—well, surprised. I thought you were *for* the slaves. I thought you *liked* it when they went North to be free."

"Oh, I do! I pray for each one of them who has the courage to go to Canada. But it's not that simple." Sarah adjusted a pin in my dress hem. "See, Papa could get put in prison or get fined as much as this whole farm is worth if anybody in his household—even a child!—was thought to have helped a slave escape. Besides, you have to think about the danger it puts the slave in. Slaves have been whipped and had their fingers or ears cut off for reading or for looking at a map! Not here at our farm, of course. But what if you taught Rissy to read a map, and then she went to another farm where her master wasn't as nice as Papa? He might even kill her for it. Do you understand?"

"I guess, but—well, it's just so *wrong*!" I blurted out.

"It's a very complicated situation," Sarah replied firmly.

I didn't see why it had to be that way. Right was right and wrong was wrong, and there wasn't anything complicated about that. But Sarah had been so kind about my crying that I didn't want to argue with her.

At least I was soon too busy to mope over not getting a letter. The next morning, Josie came down with influenza, which meant that Rissy had to do the laundry, ironing, and cloth-spinning. Clio had to do Rissy's work in the house and kitchen. Aunt Laura had to prepare the wedding invitations and nurse Josie, as well as supervise everybody else. Sarah was busy going to Miss Jenny's, and making sure she had all the linens, candles, soap, clothes, skin cream, and other things a bride needed when she moved to her new home. Uncle Henry was overseeing the field hands, and took Neddy along with him to learn how it was done. So I was the only one who could air the linens, dust the furniture, sweep the rugs, and mop the hall floor. I also molded the butter, made cheese with Aunt Laura, and helped Jupiter plant the melon patch.

Friday, Isaac and Zeke came down with influenza, too. Aunt Laura ran back and forth to the quarters with boneset tea, horehound cough drops, hot onion plasters for their chests, and hot mustard baths for their feet.

"I can fix them some spicebush tea," I offered. "It heals a person as well as boneset tea and is a lot tastier."

"No, thank you," Aunt Laura said. "I prefer using my boneset tea."

"I also know a good tonic," I told her. "You mix four cloves of garlic with dandelions, crushed pecans, and—"

"Yes, I *know* that recipe. But I don't have any pecans right now."

"Then you could use—"

"Mary *Gillian!*" my aunt cried in exasperation. "Must you be so all-fired *bossy*? I declare, you think you could run the universe all by yourself!"

I blinked at her, shocked. "I—I just wanted to help."

"You probably mean well. But," my aunt said, shaking a finger at me, "you're awfully quick to grab the reins when someone else is driving, my girl."

"I am?"

"Yes, indeedy. Now, if you really want to help, go do your mending."

"Yes, ma'am."

While I mended trousers and darned stockings, I thought about what she'd said. How dare she call me bossy—when *she* was as bossy as an old cow! Maybe she was mad because I knew as much as she did about remedies—more than she did, judging from the notes I'd found in her herb room.

"I'm not bossy, am I?" I asked Rissy that Saturday night. We were standing outside the kitchen waiting for our star to come out, and I'd just told her what Aunt Laura had said.

Rissy looked thoughtful. "I ain't meanin' no offense by sayin' this, Gilly, but I can see why Miz Hayden'd maybe think you was bossy. She's a growed-up woman, and you ain't. She might not like havin' a li'l gal-child tellin' her what to do. Might think you're showin' off, like."

"I only want to help," I said.

But I thought about it as we sat there and I guessed maybe I had been showing off some. I wanted Aunt Laura to see how smart I was. Besides, I *did* know more about remedies!

Still, maybe it wouldn't hurt to curb my tongue a little.

Tolliver hollered for Rissy while we still had our eyes closed, hugging our pas.

"I'll be right in!" she replied. Then she whispered to me, "There's food missin' again. Remember them meat pies you had for dinner day 'fore yesterday? There was half of one left, and I put it in the icehouse. But today when I went with Tolliver to put in the leftover fricasseed chicken, it was gone! I asked Tolliver what had happened to it, and he said there hadn't *been* no leftover meat pie. I said yes, there had been, and he said, 'Gal, you seein' things. First you see tater buns where there ain't no tater buns. Then you see meat pie where there ain't no meat pie. Next you gonna be seein' corn bread a-flyin' through the air and shucky beans dancin' on the tabletop. People's gonna think you crazy and lock you away.' "

"Do you think he and Clio are stealing food and eating it themselves?"

"Hmmph!" she snorted. "Them two goody-goodies? They wouldn't steal nothin' if they was starvin'."

"Then who do you think is taking it?"

"New gal, you comin' to finish these here dishes or has I gots to fetch you myself?" came Tolliver's voice.

"Comin', Tolliver!" Rissy yelled. Then she whispered again, "Maybe there is a ghost livin' up in that herb room.

I'm gonna keep watchin' things with both my eyes, and try to figure out what's goin' on."

I'd hoped everybody would get over their influenza so I could go back to working in the gardens and dairy. But Josie stayed sick, and Clio and Aunt Laura were still busy nursing people, so I had to keep doing the housework while Rissy did the washing and ironing. There was more housework than I could shake a stick at, too, since David was coming for dinner the next Sunday: the dining room furniture and floor had to be waxed, the damask table-cloth washed and ironed, the fancy salt cellars and goblets washed, and the silver dinnerware and candlesticks polished.

One morning while I was cleaning the bedrooms, I sneaked up the narrow attic stairs to look over my running-away provisions. I was proud of my little cache of goods: a sliver of soap, a few matches, my tin cup, my wooden spoon and trencher, the half eagle, and maps I'd traced from the atlas. It looked more and more as if I was going to need them. The week's mail had come, and once again there'd been no letter from Pa.

When I had time to play with Neddy on Saturday, I added something else to my collection, something that pleased me mightily: a genuine Barlow pocket knife, which I won at marbles. I had Rufus Peacock to thank for it: he'd been the champion marbles player of Prairie

Flower and had taught me how to knuckle down and flick my shooter so that it knocked the other marbles clear out of the circle.

"But girls can't play marbles!" Neddy howled.

"*I* can," I said, "although I'm used to using the eyeballs of the lions and tigers I've killed instead of clay marbles like these."

"Wow!" he breathed in admiration, and handed over his knife.

On Sunday, Sarah didn't go to church because she was too excited about David's coming. Neddy and I weren't that excited and couldn't think of any other excuse, so we climbed into the wagon with Aunt Laura and Uncle Henry.

Mr. Milkweed-Hair preached on God Smiting the Wicked, and I gave him a big smile as I pictured God smiting Aunt Laura, the Craikeys, and Tolliver. Mr. Milkweed-Hair blinked at me in surprise. I guessed he had never seen me smile during his sermons. Usually I either glared at him or nodded with boredom. I missed Rissy's singing, though. She was helping Tolliver prepare dinner for David, while Clio readied the dining room.

After the service, I heard Uncle Henry grumble to Mr. Craikey, "I'll be glad when all this wedding to-do is over with. I love that daughter of mine, but I don't have time to be in the house entertaining. I've got a farm to run! Weddings are expensive, too. I would never have gotten the house plastered last month if I'd known how much it costs to get a girl married properly."

He grimaced and went on. "Now I owe the dressmaker a fortune on top of everything else. Besides, two of my purebred cows died calving, and their calves died, too. Confound it, I was counting on selling those calves."

I didn't hear any more because Neddy called me to come jump flat-footed off the top of the church steps so we could see which of us could jump farther.

When we got home, Aunt Laura wanted me to stay dressed and not get dirty before dinner, so Neddy and I sat on his bed and played Scripture Cards. I let him win, because I was still feeling a little guilty over taking his half eagle.

David arrived about two. He and the other grownups spent an hour in the parlor talking. I couldn't hear what they were saying, but I could tell David had a nice voice.

Aunt Laura came upstairs to bring Neddy a dinner tray.

"I trust you'll mind your manners at dinner," she said to me.

"Yes, ma'am."

I might as well have said *no, ma'am*, because Aunt Laura kept on. "Don't smack your lips, don't slouch over your food, don't belch, don't take large bites, don't gesture with your fork, and don't speak unless spoken to."

"Yes, ma'am."

Behind his ma's back, Neddy was grinning and wiggling his fingers in his ears at me, since he was getting to eat upstairs while I had to go down and be polite to Sarah's beau. As I followed Aunt Laura out of the room, I turned around and stuck out my tongue at him. We both burst into giggles.

"And don't giggle, Mary Gillian."

"Yes, ma'am."

I got into the dining room just as Uncle Henry, Sarah, and David were entering from the parlor.

Sarah was blushing and beaming. "David, here's my cousin Gilly. Gilly, this is David Thurmond."

If I had been an artist and somebody had said, "Miss Bucket, paint a picture of a dashing, handsome young hero," I would have painted an exact likeness of David Thurmond. He was tall and slender, with flaxen hair and thoughtful brown eyes. His shoulders were broad, and his skin was clear and browned from the sun.

In the book *Prairie Flower*, I remembered, the heroes and their ladyloves had suffered far too much heart-fluttering, bashful blushing, trembling, and swooning for my taste. When I'd told Granny Pea that, she'd laughed and said I'd understand someday. Now, looking at David Thurmond, I realized she'd been right. I felt a butterfly where my heart should be, and I knew my face was pinkish.

David sat across from me at dinner. I was careful to use my best manners: not only to abide by all of Aunt Laura's rules, but also to dab at my mouth daintily with my napkin. I even kept quiet and listened to David and Uncle Henry talk about their crops. I thought it was unfair that they could discuss fertilizer and soil at the table, whereas I could mention only ladylike things.

"My winter wheat's growing so fast the seed heads are forming already," Uncle Henry said proudly. "It looks like an excellent crop—should be ready to harvest before the end of June. Corn's doing as well as the wheat. I'm already setting out the peas in the cornfield. The cornstalks will soon be tall enough to stake the vines to."

"I have a fine crop coming up, too." David's voice was as smooth and soft as creek water. "My field hands have been quick to pick up the farming methods I've been teaching them. They've taught *me* some things as well."

I was so surprised, I exclaimed, "I thought you didn't have slaves!"

"Mary *Gill*ian," my aunt said.

"I don't have slaves," David replied, ignoring Aunt Laura. "I hire my field hands, as well as my cook and housekeeper, and pay them. Some are whites and some are free blacks."

Uncle Henry chuckled and shook his head. "I still tell you, they'll leave when they get enough money," he said.

"If my workers are unhappy working for me, they have the right to leave," David said quietly, "just like any other free citizen."

Sarah was looking back and forth between them anxiously. "Let's discuss something else, shall we?" she asked gaily.

David smiled at her. "You're right. We shouldn't argue at the dinner table. Is the rain making your plants grow quickly, Mrs. Hayden?"

Before Aunt Laura could answer, Uncle Henry said, "Mr. Thurmond, I don't wish to argue. I just don't want you to think my people are unhappy. I treat my people well. I give them plenty of food and nice cabins to live in."

He turned to Clio, who had just come in with a platter of fresh ham. "Isn't that right, gal?"

Clio gave him a big smile. "Why, *yes*suh, Mas' Hayden. You treats us *fine*."

Uncle Henry gloated. "Hear that, Mr. Thurmond? Clio agrees with me. You can go now, gal," he added, motioning to Clio. "We'll help ourselves to the ham."

Clio set the platter on the sideboard and left.

I made a little face at her back as she went out the door. I knew she had to agree with Uncle Henry, or risk being punished. But she didn't have to be such a toady.

Uncle Henry said to David, "You Northerners don't understand that our people *need* us. We give them clothes, food, and shelter. We make sure they do their work properly. We keep them healthy and productive, even if they aren't always grateful."

Aunt Laura cleared her throat. She said quietly but earnestly, "He's right, Mr. Thurmond. You Northerners don't understand that you wouldn't do the slaves any favor by abolishing slavery. They simply couldn't manage on their own, any more than—than a child Neddy's age could."

I saw David's jaw muscles tighten and thought for a happy moment that Aunt Laura's time to be smote had come. But David simply said, "You're wrong, ma'am. They manage under more trying circumstances than you can imagine."

"Hmmph!" Uncle Henry grunted. "With all due respect, Mr. Thurmond, I never thought I'd have an abolitionist for a son-in-law. I only hope you aren't mixed up in that underground railroad nonsense."

"Would anyone like more ham?" Sarah sounded desperate.

Nobody answered.

"Excuse me, Mr. Thurmond," I said politely. I bet he'd answer the question that I didn't dare ask my aunt and uncle. "What is the underground railroad? Does it have something to do with slaves escaping?"

"Yes, it does," he answered before Aunt Laura or Uncle Henry could tell me to be quiet. "The underground railroad is a secret network of people who help the slaves get to Canada. They hide the slaves along the way and transport them from one hiding place to the next."

"So it's not a real train?"

"No." David smiled. "That's just a name. The places where the slaves are hidden are called stations, and the people in the network are stationmasters and conductors. There are a number of different routes to Canada, mostly up through Pennsylvania and New York, or northwest through Ohio and across the Great Lakes."

"Is the Spirit one of the people in the secret network?"

In his beautiful, soft voice, David said, "Yes. The Spirit is someone in this area—a stationmaster or conductor— who hides or moves runaway slaves. Nobody knows who he is. He's called the Spirit because he 'spirits' the slaves away."

Aunt Laura sniffed. "Spirit, hmmph! *Pirate* is more like it!"

"Ought to be hanged, that's what I say!" Uncle Henry put in. "Doesn't he know that our people are our property? He's no better than a common horse thief!"

I had to speak my thoughts, even if it meant reading Job for a whole month. "My pa says it's not right for one human being to own another one. I think the Spirit is a good man, and I hope he doesn't get caught."

"Mary Gillian!" Aunt Laura gasped. "Mr. Thurmond,

please forgive my niece for speaking out of turn. Perhaps she had better go upstairs now."

"No, please, Mrs. Hayden, let her stay," David urged. "We shouldn't be arguing at the dinner table. Besides, Gilly can't help voicing her opinions. She's a spitfire."

I was so delighted I nearly dropped my fork. A spitfire. I liked the sound of that.

Aunt Laura gave me a warning look and said, "Very well, Mr. Thurmond, if you insist and if she promises to behave herself."

"I'm certain she will," David replied, smiling at me. "Gilly, I'm glad you think the Spirit's a good man and don't want him to be caught. He'd be grateful to you, whoever he is."

He winked at me.

"Can we talk about something else now?" Sarah asked.

"Yes, let's do," Aunt Laura said. "Tell me, Mr. Thurmond, what day will your family arrive?"

As they chatted, I went over David's words in my mind. And that wink! It was as though he'd been sharing a secret with me—something he wanted only me to know and hoped I'd be clever enough to figure out.

Well, I was clever enough to figure it out, and the realization was so powerful it almost knocked me off my chair: *David Thurmond was the Spirit!* That was what he'd been trying to tell me!

I looked at him across the table as he conversed politely with Aunt Laura. He was young, gallant, and brave. He was calm and intelligent. He didn't believe in slavery. He even had family in New York who could be conductors and stationmasters up there.

He *had* to be the Spirit!

I couldn't wait to tell Rissy all I'd learned: The underground railroad wasn't even a real train. Best of all, the Spirit was as dashing and handsome a hero as anyone could want—and he was my own cousin's bridegroom!

8

RISSY WAS AS EXCITED AS I WAS.

"So you're sayin' that train ain't no train at all!" she marveled as we stood whispering in the dining room after breakfast. "It's a string of folks passin' us along up to Canada. I guess I'm kinda happy to hear that. I was worried about that train goin' underground through folks' buryin' places and all. And you say Miz Sarah's beau's the Spirit?"

"He didn't come out and say so," I said. "But I'm sure he is."

"I just saw him for a second when he was comin' in. He sure is a handsome fella! You think Miz Sarah knows he's the Spirit?"

Before I could answer, Aunt Laura came in. She eyed us disapprovingly.

"Rissy, here's a cone of sugar for you to give Tolliver," she said. "You'd best go back to the kitchen now. Neither of you has time to be socializing."

"Yes, ma'am," we said together, as though we'd rehearsed it.

Rissy's question was something I'd been asking inside my head. Did Sarah know that David was the Spirit? And if she didn't, what would she do when she found out? I remembered how upset she had been when she'd seen Rissy and me looking at the atlas.

While we were sewing that afternoon, I asked thoughtfully, "Sarah, suppose you found out somebody was hiding a slave. Somebody you cared a lot about. Would you tell on him?"

"Well, not if I cared about him, I guess. Would you hand me those scissors, please?"

I gave her the little thread-snipping scissors.

"But what if this somebody needed you to *help*?" I persisted. "What if the slave was sick or was a little child and needed your care? Or what if you knew where a slave was hidden, and some big tough men came to your door and demanded that you tell them? Would you do it?"

"Gilly, *I* don't know! Why are you asking me these things?" Sarah tugged on her needle. "Oh, this dratted thread is tangled again! Maybe there's a better spool of blue thread in the sewing basket."

Sarah, I thought sadly, wouldn't be any help at all to

the Spirit. She was the kindest girl in the world, but—well, she wasn't a spitfire.

I thought I'd worked hard the week before, but that was nothing compared to how hard I worked in the days before Sarah's wedding. Everything in the house had to be washed, polished, dusted, trimmed, swept, shaken, scrubbed, rearranged, or hung outside to freshen.

I had to admit that Aunt Laura was busy, too. She seemed to be everywhere at once: mixing the lye-and-soap solution for me to polish the silver with; helping Clio wash the downstairs windows; clipping herbs; making sure Neddy hadn't outgrown his suit; caring for the sick people; and, of course, finding something wrong with everything I did.

"I hope you're doing a thorough job on the good silverware," she said at the dinner table on Tuesday. "I don't want those New York people saying my silver is dull."

"Yes, ma'am. I mean, they won't, ma'am. I'm polishing it until I can look in the spoon backs and count the freckles on my face."

That got a little chuckle from her. "I suppose that's satisfactory," she said.

Rissy was ironing clothes in the laundry room, where I was polishing the silver. "We're havin' our ball Saturday night," she said. "It was gonna be the night before Miz Sarah's weddin', but if we have it Saturday, Mas' Craikey's people can come, too. That big old cabin at the end of the row is empty, and Dilsey says Mas' Hayden lets us have it for dances. It's got a real wood floor! That means we can pat out the rhythms with our feet while we're dancin'. Jupiter's gonna play his fiddle, and a man from Mas' Craikey's is bringin' his gourd flute. We're gonna dance all night!"

"Can I come, too?" I asked eagerly. "I loved to dance when we had parties back home."

Rissy hesitated, then shook her head. She said shyly, "It wouldn't be right, Gilly. See, if folks knew a white gal was watchin', they'd feel all stiff and starchy-like. A body can't do much dancin' feelin' like that."

"Umm." Embarrassed, I bent my head and rubbed a silver fork with the polishing rag. Sometimes I forgot about being a white gal. "Do you think Clio will bring her beau?"

"You know, it's real funny," Rissy said. "I asked her that same thing, and she looked at me like I was crazy. She said, 'I ain't got no beau, gal. What you be talkin' about?' I didn't want to tell her I'd noticed her bein' gone in the night, so I just said I was jokin'."

I giggled. "Maybe her beau's ugly and she doesn't want anybody to see him."

"Or she might be afraid he'd get whupped if he's Mas' Craikey's and somebody found out he's been sneakin' out at night."

Rissy unrolled Sarah's green silk party dress to iron. "Lordy, I wish I had a dress like this to wear to the dance!" she said.

She held it up to her and sashayed around, singing, "Goin' to the ball, dee-di-di-diddle!"

"Rissy, I know what!" I cried. "Sarah has a whole trunk full of party clothes in the attic. That's where I got my blue dress for the wedding. I'll bet she'd give you a dress, too."

"You think she would?" Rissy's face was full of joy. "Clio and Dilsey've got dresses from Miz Hayden. Sarah, though, she'd be nearer my size."

"I'll ask her," I promised.

I did it that afternoon, when I tried on my own new dress.

"It fits perfectly!" Sarah pronounced, standing back and looking at me. "You're going to look lovely, Gilly, once we get your hair combed and some shoes on your feet."

I wasn't sure I'd look lovely, but I guessed I'd look closer to it than usual. And I'd get to show off my pendant.

Sarah thought it was a wonderful idea to give Rissy some of her old dresses, so later in the week we went up to the attic to look at them again. A few were too heavy to wear for dancing in the summertime, but the prettiest one of all—a rose-red one with five flounces on the skirt—was a lightweight silk. Sarah and I took that one, a lilac poplin with black trim, and a pink silk with a wide sash out to the kitchen to Rissy.

"Oh, Miz Sarah, ma'am!" Rissy cried when she saw them. "Are they all three for me?"

"Yes," Sarah said, smiling. "I have some heavier ones you can have for winter."

"Thank you, Miz Sarah." Rissy curtsied, and looked down at the floor, overwhelmed with bashfulness.

"I'll take them to your cabin," I said. "You can try them on later and decide which one to wear Saturday night."

"Thank you, Gilly—uh, *Miz* Gilly," Rissy corrected, glancing at Sarah.

"Have a good time at the ball," Sarah said. "Tolliver, bake me a lovely wedding cake!"

"Yes'm, Miz Sarah," Tolliver said proudly. "I's gonna make you a French almond cake, and that's the best cake there is. I ain't about to stint none on it, neither. I's gonna use fourteen eggs and soak them almonds in rose water to make it extra good."

"Umm, it sounds delicious. I can't wait to taste it," Sarah replied with a smile. "Now we'll get out of your way, so you can get on with your work. Come along, Gilly."

I saw Rissy beaming with happiness as she bent over the pot she was stirring. I was dying to talk to her.

"We can visit on Sunday afternoon," she whispered when we passed each other in the dining room the next morning. "Clio's gonna work then."

"We'll go to the woods," I whispered back.

Saturday night, I lay in my trundle bed and stared into the darkness long after Sarah had gone to sleep. Through the open window, I heard Jupiter's fiddle playing for the dance.

I got up and went to the window. For a long time, I looked out at the stars and listened to the fiddling, laughing, and rhythmic clapping that came from the quarters. I wished I was there.

Suddenly I saw something moving between the dairy and the laundry. There was only a little sliver of a moon, and I wouldn't have seen anything if my eyes hadn't adjusted to the darkness already. I saw the laundry room door open and close and, a minute later, I saw the tiny flame of a candle through the kitchen window.

It must be Tolliver, I thought. But why had he left his room over the dairy and gone into the kitchen at this time of night? And why hadn't he taken a lantern?

The little candle flame disappeared, as though someone had blown it out or hidden it.

I watched for a long time, but I didn't see any more lights or movements. Was Tolliver working in the kitchen in the dark? And if so, why?

I finally got too sleepy to watch any longer, and went back to bed.

Rissy wore her red silk dress to church. She had her hair out of its usual scarf, and hanging down stiff and straight to her shoulders.

"You looked beautiful!" I told her when we met in the woods that afternoon.

"Thank you," she said, patting her hair self-consciously. "Dilsey washed my hair with rainwater and laundry bluing, then straightened it with a hot knife."

She reached into her pocket and handed me a scrap of paper. "Here," she said. "I made you a present, to thank you for askin' Sarah about the dresses."

In large, neat letters, it said: RISSY HAS THREE NEW DRESSES.

"I wrote it myself," she said proudly. "Is it all right?"

"It's perfect!" I hugged her.

She told me about the dance in so much detail that I felt as if I'd been there.

"I heard the music and laughing." I added, "I also saw Tolliver."

I told her about Tolliver's mysterious trip to the kitchen, and she was as puzzled as I was.

"There's more food disappearin', too," she said. "Some biscuits and sausage from breakfast this mornin' went missin', and so did a couple o' taters from dinner. I've been countin' things and payin' attention, but I ain't sayin' nothin' to Tolliver or Clio. I'll just bide my time until you and I can figure out who's to blame."

"What'll we do then?" I asked.

She shrugged. "Guess we gotta figure that out when we see who it is."

We read and wrote and talked until Rissy had to go help prepare supper.

"Clio's feelin' a little poorly," she said, "so she asked me to serve at the table tonight. I hope she just partied too late and ain't gettin' sick like Josie and them. After all, Miz Sarah's weddin's the day after tomorrow."

But Clio felt more and more poorly, and that night Aunt Laura diagnosed her as having influenza.

"Of all the times for her to get sick!" my aunt exclaimed at breakfast. She clinked her teacup into the saucer and said, "Rissy, you aren't going to take sick, are you?"

"No, ma'am." Rissy turned around from setting the covered pewter bowl on the sideboard. "I had the influenza already, when I was at Mas' Percy's."

"Well, thank goodness for that," my aunt said. "We'll all have to work extra as it is."

That afternoon, Aunt Laura and I helped Sarah gather, sort, and pack the things to be sent to her new home and the clothes she would take on her honeymoon. On Tuesday, Neddy and I did Clio's share of the cleaning. Rissy took broth and medicine to the invalids and helped Tolliver, who was baking the wedding cake. Aunt Laura supervised Uncle Henry and Jupiter as they moved the smaller pieces of furniture from the parlor, where the ceremony was to be held, into the library. Uncle Henry bumped into a chair that he'd left in the hallway, lost his temper, and hollered about how much money this dratted wedding was costing him. Sarah heard him, burst into tears, and ran to her room. Aunt Laura went upstairs to console her.

That night everybody took baths, and Sarah washed my hair with eggs and rum again. She was very quiet, and I wondered if she was having second thoughts about marrying David, or felt bad because Uncle Henry had carried on so about the expense.

While the eggs stiffened on my hair, I said, "It's going to be a real pretty wedding and Mr. Thurmond's so handsome and all. You sure must be happy."

"Oh, Gilly," my cousin said in a trembling voice. She sniffled and reached for her little bird-sneeze handkerchief. "Do you realize that soon I'll be a married woman?"

"Isn't that what you want?"

"Yes. But—well, I don't know *how*."

"How to what?" I asked uneasily. I hoped she didn't mean how to get a baby started in her stomach. I didn't think I could explain it as well as Granny Pea had.

"I don't know how to run a household," she said.

I was relieved, but I still didn't understand.

She explained, "At school I learned how to play the piano and speak French and embroider, and Mama taught me how to sew and make preserves. But I don't know the first thing about keeping an account book, or planning menus, or supervising servants."

I shrugged. "Just write down what you spend, and tell the servants what you'd like to eat and what you want them to do."

"It's not that simple," my cousin replied sadly, shaking her head. "I have to keep track of all the household money—how much David gives me, how much I give the servants to buy our food, and how much change they give back. I have to keep up with how much things cost so I'll know whether the servants are cheating us. I have to plan ahead so we won't run out of money. As for menus, I have to know what vegetables are in season, how long it will take the cook to prepare various dishes, what sauces and gravies to order for what meats, and what foods David likes. I have to keep an inventory of the meats in the smokehouse, the vegetables in the cellar, and the jams and spices in the pantry. I have to learn how to talk to the servants so they'll like and respect me. David thinks his cook and housekeeper are wonderful."

"Then they can help you," I said.

"But they might dislike me and quit, or laugh at me. Besides," she added, wrinkling her nose, "I'll have to oversee the butchering in the fall, and I might have to be-head a chicken. I don't think I can do those things without fainting, Gilly! And there's more. When the servants get sick, I'll have to nurse them—and I'm not an expert at cures like Mama. Also, if we're shorthanded, I might have to milk a cow or start the kitchen fire or scrub clothes. I don't know how to do any of those things."

"I do," I said. "I also know how to inventory food and decide what to fix for supper. I used to help Granny Pea. After you get married, I could come visit you and teach you. That is, I could if—"

I'd almost said, *if I weren't running off to find Pa*. Instead I ended with, "if you wouldn't think I was being bossy."

"Why ever would I think that?" Sarah cried. "Would you really come? Mama offered to, but I'm afraid she and David would argue."

"I'd love to come."

Sarah pulled a strand of my hair out straight to see whether the egg whites had done what they were supposed to yet.

She clucked her tongue. "At least I'm luckier than Mama was when she married Papa."

"Why?" I asked.

"Well . . . because David and I are in *love*. I think your mama, Aunt Mary Kate, was in love, too, since she went off with your papa against her parents' wishes. But I don't think Mama and Papa were in love. Once, when I was little, I asked Mama how they'd met, and she said their fathers were friends and wanted them to marry. She kind of laughed and said, 'I was nearly twenty and didn't have any prospects. Your grandpa was afraid I'd be an old maid and wanted me married off.' That didn't sound to me like she and Papa were in love. But don't you tell anybody I said that!"

"I won't," I promised.

That didn't keep me from ruminating on it, though. It must be awful to marry someone you hadn't chosen, knowing you'd be stuck with him forever. I supposed you might grow to love him over the years. Still, that wouldn't be the same as having a spark lit in your bosom.

Maybe that was one reason Aunt Laura didn't smile much, I thought, watching her that night as she straightened the tablecloth for the hundredth time. *I* wasn't going to get married until I met someone whose very glance set my heart aflame and filled me with golden rapture, the way it happened in the novels I'd read. Someone like, say, David Thurmond.

After our baths, we went to bed early. We were so clean and the house was so tidy we didn't know what else to do.

When I woke up the next morning, Sarah was sitting on her bed, brushing her hair.

"Morning, Gilly," she said. She smiled a nervous smile. "It's my wedding day."

"It's a nice, sunny day," I told her. "That's good luck."

The wedding was to be at eleven o'clock. After breakfast, I sat on Sarah's bed and watched as Aunt Laura took the curling tongs and crimping iron to my cousin's hair. Then she helped Sarah dress. First came silk stockings, then a tightly laced corset. A cage of hoops was fastened around Sarah's waist to support her skirt. Each hoop was wider than the one above it, and they were held together by ribbons running down each side. Over that went the bride's dress itself, a creation of white satin and lace.

Sarah looked beautiful, but I was glad I didn't have to be crimped, laced, and hooped. After Aunt Laura left, I put on my blue dress, lifted my pendant over the bodice, slipped on my shoes, and ran a comb through my hair. I was ready.

As I went downstairs, I heard voices in the parlor: Aunt Laura's bossy one, Sarah's nervous one, and David's deep, calm one. The wedding party must be rehearsing! I wanted to watch, but there was a flowered silk folding screen in front of the parlor doorway. I got down on the floor and peered underneath. All I could see was feet and hems—not enough to be worth the scolding I'd get if Aunt Laura saw me.

Disappointed, I went out to the front porch and sat on the steps beside Neddy, who looked as cute as a chipmunk in his short pants and jacket. Since we couldn't play tag or make mud pies, we played a game of guessing which wedding guests would arrive first. Neddy said it would be Dr. Granger. I said David's parents.

I won. David's parents got there at ten-thirty. The other guests soon followed: Dr. Granger, Mr. and Mrs. Craikey, several people I had seen in church, and a few I had never seen. As people came up the steps, Neddy told them firmly that they were to stay on the porch until Uncle Henry opened the front door. Everyone chuckled and a few guests patted him on the head, but they did as he said.

As the adults stood and chatted, I noticed that one woman, tall, with a beak nose and high-swept brown hair, kept looking at me. At first it irked me, but finally I looked right back at her and grinned, just to see what she'd do. To my surprise, her face broke into a glorious smile and she came over to me.

"Are you Mary Kate Madison's daughter?" she asked.

"Yes, ma'am. I'm Mary Gillian Bucket."

"I knew it!" She clasped her hands. "I'm Miss Emma Bussy."

I nodded. "Aunt Laura's friend from Richmond. Did you know my ma?"

"Yes, I did, although I was mostly your aunt's friend. Mary Kate was a lot younger than us, and very ladylike. She always had pretty clothes and little boys chasing her."

"Ma did?" I remembered Ma as pretty and well mannered, but I'd never pictured her as an eastern young lady with nice dresses and beaux.

Miss Bussy lifted my pendant and chuckled. "My, this brings back memories. I noticed it as soon as I saw you. That's how I knew you must be Laura's niece. I suppose she told you the story—or the family legend, I should say!"

"Family legend? No, ma'am."

"She never told you about the time she threw this in the creek?"

"The creek?" I gaped at her. "Aunt Laura?"

"Oh, yes!" Miss Bussy patted my arm. "It looks like the ceremony is about to start. We'll chat more later."

I wanted to chat more right then, to find out about Aunt Laura throwing my pendant into the creek. But Uncle Henry was opening the front door and inviting everyone inside. The folding screen had been removed, and my uncle escorted David's parents into the parlor. The rest of us stood in the wide hallway. Dr. Granger made a place for Neddy and me in front, so we could see the ceremony instead of people's backsides.

In the parlor, the wedding party was in place. David and Sarah stood facing Mr. Milkweed-Hair. Beside David was a young man, who I supposed was the best man. Sarah's lovely maid of honor had the same flaxen hair and brown eyes as David, so I guessed she was his sister Olivia, who had gone to school with Sarah. She wore a white dress with a pink sash and held a bouquet of pink flowers that complemented the pink, salmon, and pale yellow blooms that Aunt Laura had arranged in cut-glass vases to decorate the room.

Aunt Laura, Uncle Henry, and David's parents sat on the sofa. Uncle Henry looked hot and grouchy in his suit. Aunt Laura looked nicer than usual, in a deep green silk dress with a cameo brooch at the neck. Her glance fell on my pendant, and I tried not to smirk.

The ceremony took hardly any time at all. Mr. Milkweed-Hair read from the Bible and had David and Sarah exchange rings. David looked solemn. Sarah cried a little. To my amazement, Aunt Laura gave a sniffle and dabbed her eyes with a handkerchief. Even Uncle Henry's mouth quivered a bit.

Neddy didn't cry; he got the hiccups.

"Think of a fox with no tail," I whispered. That was the best hiccups cure I knew.

He scrunched up his face and thought hard, and it worked.

Mr. Milkweed-Hair asked God to give the new Mr. and Mrs. Thurmond a long life together and a house full of children. I silently asked Him to also please help Sarah learn to cook and clean and, even more important, to help her become a spitfire who could help David in his Spirit work.

After the ceremony, first Aunt Laura and then everyone else went up to congratulate the new couple. I wanted to find Miss Bussy and hear about Aunt Laura and my pendant, but I didn't see her. I hoped she hadn't forgotten me and left early.

Rissy brought in a pitcher of lemonade and motioned for me to follow her out into the back yard.

Outside, she said in a low voice, "That ol' Mas' Craikey saw me settin' out the wine bottles earlier. He sidled up and said, real flirty-like, 'Where's that red dress you had on at church?' I didn't answer, and he said, 'You're as purty as a speckled pup and you sing as purty as a bird. You know that?' I still didn't say anything. He got mad and said, 'You think you're too good to talk to me, slave gal? If you were mine, I'd whup you till you talked!' Then he looked me over, nasty-like, and said, 'That wouldn't be *all* I'd do to you, neither.' "

"Rissy, that's awful!"

She shuddered. "I don't like him bein' anywhere close to me."

"You ought to tell Uncle Henry what he said," I told her.

She shook her head. "Mas' Craikey's his friend. He might not believe me."

"Still, you have to—"

The kitchen door slammed. Tolliver stood there, his arms crossed.

"You better be gettin' your skinny li'l old self back in here, new gal. There's guests in that house, if you ain't noticed."

I crossed my arms and glared back at him. "Her name isn't new gal, it's Clarissa Ruth. And we have important things to discuss."

"Well, you better make 'em important and quick," Tolliver said, and went back inside.

"I'll tell Uncle Henry about Mr. Craikey," I said.

"No, Gilly, that'd just make things worse!" she cried. "I'll tell him myself—but not until tomorrow morning, after the weddin's all over with."

"All right, but if you don't talk to him in the morning, I will," I told her.

When I got back inside, everyone was in the library, watching Uncle Henry write an entry in the Hayden family Bible.

"On this day," he read aloud, "Sarah Elizabeth Hayden married David Thomas Thurmond. June 1, 1859."

I heard Aunt Laura sniffle again.

The others went into the hallway to have more cake and lemonade, but I lingered over the old Bible. Like the Bucket family Bible upstairs in my trunk, this one had been used to record all the family births, weddings, and deaths for many years. Of Uncle Henry's parents, the entries said: "Henry Edward Hayden II departed to join his

Father in Heaven on August 16, 1847," and "Elizabeth Boyer Hayden departed to join her Father in Heaven on December 6, 1848."

I thought, Mary Gillian Bucket will depart to join her father in the Rocky Mountains on June 15 or thereabouts, 1859.

A lilting voice behind me said, "Ah, there you are, Mary Gillian."

I looked around. It was Miss Bussy.

"I went outside to get some air," she said, "but I wanted to see you again before I left."

"Tell me about Aunt Laura and my pendant!" I cried. Then I added, "Please, ma'am."

"Well, it happened right after your great-aunt gave it to your mother. Laura and I were about your age. She had always loved that pendant, and said her great-aunt had promised to give it to her someday. But her great-aunt was old and forgetful, and like everybody else, she had more fondness for pretty Mary Kate. So she gave the pendant to her instead. Laura was furious. She took it when nobody was looking, ran into the woods, and threw it into the creek behind her parents' house."

"Aunt Laura did that? Are you sure?"

Miss Bussy had a nice, tinkly laugh. "Yes. Afterward, she got scared of what she'd done and came running to me for help. She was all muddy and crying. We looked for hours, but we couldn't find the pendant."

"How did it get found?" I asked.

"Your grandma accused Mary Kate of having lost it, and Mary Kate cried and insisted she hadn't. Laura finally confessed. Your grandpa went out the next day and searched the creek until he found it. Laura was so miserable she got off with just a talking-to. Your grandpa said both girls were too young to have such nice jewelry. He took the pendant and locked it up."

"When did Ma get it back?"

She replied, "Not until she was—what? Sixteen, I guess. It was when she told your grandparents she was going to marry your pa and move out to Missouri. They were beside themselves. They didn't approve of their precious younger daughter marrying a blacksmith, even though he was book-learned and very polite. And they certainly didn't want her going out to Missouri with him! Your grandpa threatened to disown her, but he forgave her at the last minute. He gave her the pendant in case she needed money to—" Miss Bussy stopped abruptly.

"To leave Pa and come back home?"

"Yes. But of course she didn't. She was a very happy girl, out there in Missouri with your father. Laura and I read her letters over and over, and talked about how exciting her life was."

"Really?"

"Oh, yes. We were dull and settled by then. I was a spinster, living at home and taking care of my parents, and

Laura had a husband and child and a household to run. My, we were envious of Mary Kate." Miss Bussy smiled. "It's funny how things turned out: ladylike Mary Kate going out West, and adventurous hoyden Laura staying here. She must love to hear you talk about your life out on the prairie."

"Oh—why, yes, ma'am. I—I talk about it a lot."

Neddy appeared at the door. "Mama wants me to tell everybody that Sarah and David are getting ready to leave, and that you'd better hurry if you want to see them."

"We'll be right there." Miss Bussy put her hand on my arm. "You must come for tea before I return to Richmond, and we'll chat more."

I smiled. Was I dreaming? Had she really said that Aunt Laura had been a hoyden, like me? And that she'd wanted my pendant so much she'd thrown it in the creek when it went to Ma instead of her?

I squeezed into the crowd on the porch in time to see Sarah and David come out, hand in hand, still wearing their wedding clothes. Sarah stopped to hug Neddy and me.

"Promise to come visit me, Gilly," she said. "I'm going to miss you an awful lot."

"I'll miss you, too," I said, hugging her so hard that the lace of her dress bit into my arms. All of a sudden I realized just how much I'd miss her, and I gave a big sob. I couldn't help it, even though David Thurmond was right there watching.

"Don't cry," Sarah said, patting my hair. "You'll be coming to visit us as soon as we get back. You have to teach me how to keep house, remember?"

I nodded. But I knew that by the time she got back, I'd be on my way to the Rockies.

"Don't make a scene, Mary Gillian," Aunt Laura said dryly. "Sarah will be right down the road. She's not moving to China."

"Here, take this, Gilly," David said, putting a nice-sized handkerchief into my hand.

"Thank you." I blew my nose.

"Are you okay now?" he asked solemnly.

"I'm all right." I held out the handkerchief to him.

"You can keep it until you come visit us," he said.

"Okay," I said, but I hoped he'd forget I had it. I wanted to keep it always, to remember him by. "Have a good time in New York. And, uh, *good luck in your work.*" I gave him a meaningful look so he'd know I meant his work as the Spirit.

He blinked at me. "Why, thank you! That's kind of you."

I hoped he understood. He probably did, I thought, and just couldn't let on when there were so many people around.

The guests left soon after that. Miss Bussy squeezed my hand and said she was happy to have met me. Mr. Craikey blew cigar smoke in my face, and Mrs. Craikey quickly turned her eyes from me, as if she was scared I'd put a hex on her. Mr. Milkweed-Hair told me to try to be good, but he didn't sound very hopeful. Dr. Granger asked me how the herb garden was doing.

As the doctor was leaving, I thought I heard him say quietly to Aunt Laura, "Change the proportions on that motherwort tea, from six and one to six and four." But that didn't make any sense, and I decided I must have heard wrong.

When everybody had gone, I got a leftover chocolate-nut meringue and sprawled in the parlor chair to eat it.

"You don't have time to be sitting down, Mary Gillian. There's cleaning up to be done."

"Yes, ma'am. Aunt Laura," I said slowly, "do you—"

"Do I what? And don't brush those crumbs onto the floor!"

I wanted to ask her if she remembered throwing my pendant into the creek or being envious of Ma for marrying Pa and going out to live on the prairie. But I knew she'd tell me to stop being ridiculous and start doing my chores. So I said, "Oh, nothing."

Still, all the time we were gathering wineglasses and sweeping up cake crumbs, I gave her little sideways looks and thought about the things Miss Bussy had told me.

9

I TRIED TO SLEEP in Sarah's bed that night, but it was so soft I felt as if I was going to sink into the feathers and disappear. After a while I pulled out my trundle bed and got into that. Even then I was awake for a long time, because I had so much to think about: the amazing things Miss Bussy had said about Aunt Laura and Ma; the way Mr. Craikey had spoken to Rissy; the strange directions Dr. Granger kept giving my aunt for making remedies; and the surprise poor Sarah would get when she found out that her new husband was the Spirit.

Eventually I drifted off to sleep, but noises from outside woke me at dawn. They sounded like men's voices, but Uncle Henry had told everybody to sleep late this morning, so I didn't know who would be up so early.

I tried to go back to sleep, but as soon as the talking noises stopped, the birds started singing. They must be having a contest to see who could wake up the most people, I thought as I listened to the chorus of trilling, chirping, twittering, and cheeping.

Giving up the idea of sleep, I got up and went to look out the window. The sky was the palest of blues, turning gradually into peach near the eastern horizon. Wispy pink clouds, looking like torn lace, showed where the sun would rise.

Already there was smoke coming from the kitchen chimney. Rissy was the one who got up and made the fire in the mornings. That meant if I got dressed and went out there now, we could talk until Tolliver came in to start cooking breakfast. I could tell her about Miss Bussy, and I could urge her again to tell Uncle Henry what Mr. Craikey had said.

I put on my unmentionables and faded plaid dress, brushed my teeth, and rubbed my face with some water, then padded down the stairs and out the back door.

To my surprise, it was Josie's wide back, not Rissy's slender one, that I saw squatting in front of the fireplace. "Josie?" I called softly so as not to startle her. "I thought you were sick."

She looked around, still on her haunches. "Miz Gilly! What's you doin' up so early? Yes'm, I still be kinda poorly, but Rissy come knockin' on my door and say I have to help Tolliver this mornin'. She'd done lit the fire and peeled the taters already."

"But where is she? Why isn't she here?"

Josie shrugged her big shoulders. "I don't know, Miz Gilly. She didn't seem none too peart. I figured she must have got the influenza and was takin' to bed."

"She already had influenza, before she came here," I said.

"Well, maybe she done got it again," Josie said. "You ought to go look in her cabin anyways. I don't know where else she'd be."

"Okay. Thanks, Josie."

As I walked down the path to the quarters, I felt one of Rissy's worry worms come to life inside me. I wasn't sure what I was scared of, but I sure hoped I'd find Rissy tucked up in bed.

Only Clio was in the cabin. She was in bed, but awake.

"I'm sorry to bother you while you're sick," I told her, "but I'm looking for Rissy."

"Rissy?" She paused, blinking her eyes sleepily. "Ain't she up at the kitchen, helpin' with breakfast?"

"No. Josie said Rissy told her to help with breakfast this morning." The worry worm was bigger now, twisting and turning in my innards. "Do you know where she might be?"

"No'm. Sorry, Miz Gilly. I've been sleepin' the sleep

159

of the sick, and didn't wake up till a few minutes ago. I hope Rissy's all right."

"Me too. Thanks, Clio."

I fairly ran back to the kitchen, my heart pounding with a nameless fear.

This time, Tolliver was there. He was dropping chunks of onion and potato into a three-legged iron skillet that sat over hot coals raked onto the stone floor. Josie was stirring a bowl of batter.

"Tolliver, have you seen Rissy?" I asked, hearing the panic in my voice.

He looked at me sharply and pursed his lips. "No use askin' me about that gal. You go ask Mas' Hayden."

"Mas'—you mean, Uncle Henry? Tolliver, *what's happened?*"

Tolliver turned his attention back to the frying pan and said firmly, "I ain't sayin' nothin'. It be up to Mas' Hayden to tell you."

I gave a wild sob and ran back to the cabin. Clio was asleep now, but I saw what I needed to know: Rissy's three new dresses were still there, hanging on hooks, but her shoes, hairbrush, and extra hair scarf were gone.

"She's gone, too," I whispered to myself. But where?

Uncle Henry had needed money. Simon Craikey had wanted to buy Rissy.

I stood outside the cabin for a long time, sick and confused. Dilsey and Isaac came out to see if I was all right. I just said yes.

"You might want to get back in bed, child," Dilsey said kindly. "You're all pale and shaky-lookin'. You want me to help you up to the big house?"

"No, thank you," I said woodenly. "I can go by myself."

I got to the house as Uncle Henry, Aunt Laura, and Neddy were sitting down to breakfast. Josie had already set the table and served the potatoes, ham, and waffles.

"Ah, Gilly," my uncle said. "We've been wondering where you were."

I heard my own voice, low and even. "You sold Rissy."

I saw him look at Aunt Laura.

He cleared his throat and said, "Yes, I did. I was going to tell you after breakfast. But she's right down the road, at the Craikeys'. You'll still see her at church. I'll even ask Simon if you can visit her once in a while on Saturdays."

"Don't you know—" I said in that same cold voice. "Don't you know how Mr. Craikey treats his people? How he whips them? How he uses his women?"

"Don't be ridiculous," Uncle Henry said irritably. "I know Simon disciplines his people more harshly than I do, but so do most men. As for him—*ahem!*—using his women, I don't see any reason why I should discuss that with you."

I stared at him in disbelief.

"Gilly, sit down and eat your breakfast. Simon offered me eight hundred dollars for that girl, which was a lot more than she's worth. I couldn't refuse, not with all the bills I have."

I saw Rissy's proud face as she handed me the piece of paper where she'd written *Rissy has three new dresses.* I heard her singing, laughing, reading aloud. I remembered her shyly telling me how she sent her love to her daddy on a star.

More than she's *worth*?

I went crazy. I stamped my foot and screamed, *"I hate you, I hate you, I hate you!"* I hollered swearwords and obscenities at my uncle, words I hadn't even known I knew. I called him names that Rufus Peacock would have blushed to hear.

Uncle Henry jumped up so suddenly that his chair fell over backward. "That's enough, Mary Gillian! You're coming out to the barn with me."

"Papa, don't hit Gilly!"

"Be quiet, Neddy. Come along, Mary Gillian."

He dragged me outside by one arm. No matter how much I twisted and fought, I couldn't get away. He took me out to the barn and gave me a licking with a hickory switch. It hurt like fire, but I didn't cry. I just gritted my teeth and thought about how much I hated him.

Afterward, we sat down, me very carefully, on milking stools.

"Understand one thing," he said to me sternly. "No child who lives in my house is going to use that kind of language. *Ever. No matter what.*"

"But I *don't* live in your house," I retorted. "I'm just staying here until I run off to—"

I stopped, realizing too late what I'd said.

Uncle Henry cocked an eyebrow. "Until you run off? Is that what I heard you say?"

I looked down at my lap for a few seconds. Then I raised my chin stubbornly, looked at him, and said, "Yes, sir."

My uncle was silent for a moment.

"Is that how you were going to thank your aunt and me," he asked slowly, "for taking you in, looking after you, feeding and clothing you, taking you to church, trying to teach you manners? By running off?"

"I have to go find Pa."

"To go find your *pa*?" He sounded incredulous. "Do you know how far it is to the Rocky Mountains, where your pa is?"

"Fifteen hundred miles."

"And how were you planning to get fifteen hundred miles on your own?"

"Walk. Sleep in the woods. Eat fish and leaves."

"Oh, Gilly." He sighed. "Did you really believe you could do that?"

"Of course! I'm brave."

He looked at me for a long moment, then said, "There's a difference between being brave and being rash, Gilly. Surely you must see how foolish your idea was. You wouldn't make it halfway to Ohio before you'd be picked up and put in a local orphanage. Besides, how did you intend to carry the supplies and provisions you'd need? What were you going to do if you got sick or snakebit or broke your leg? How were you planning to get firewood if it rained? And did you honestly think you'd get the strength to walk that far by eating fish and leaves?"

I could only look down at the floor and shrug. My idea did seem foolish now, and my little store of provisions seemed downright pitiful.

"There's something else, too," Uncle Henry continued. "How did you intend to find your father once you got to the Rockies? Did you think you could walk around the mining camps by yourself and go climbing in places that are dangerous even for grown men? And what were you going to do if you didn't find your father or if you found out he'd been killed?"

"But he *can't* have been killed! I won't believe that!"

"Your pa's been gone since last summer." Uncle Henry's voice was gentler now. "Gilly, I'm sorry, but you have to face the facts. Your pa's been gone a long time, and nobody knows where he is. He went to a rough country and it's very possible he's been—"

"Stop!" I put my hands over my ears. "It's not true! I won't listen!"

Uncle Henry grabbed my hands and held them.

"It's very possible he's been killed. If not, then he may have decided not to send for you. He may think it's better for everyone concerned if you stay here with us."

I shook my head, furious. "No, he *wouldn't* think that!"

I tried to wrestle my hands free, but Uncle Henry held them firmly. He spoke slowly and carefully, as though I was hard of hearing. "*Gilly, your pa lost his money gambling.* It wasn't stolen. He lost it gambling. Your neighbors in Prairie Flower wrote and told us."

"It's not true! Besides, he's going to get rich finding gold and then he can pay off—"

My uncle was shaking his head sadly. "I've heard about those gold mines in the Rockies. The stories about gold there are greatly exaggerated. Very few men have found any gold at all. Most of the lucky ones have found barely enough to pay for their trip home."

"But maybe he was *very* lucky and—"

"You have to face reality, Gilly. You live here with us, and you may as well settle down and start behaving like a young lady. If you don't, I'll send you to a strict boarding school until you're old enough to be married off. Is that clear?"

"Y-yes, sir." At least he hadn't said an orphanage. But a strict boarding school! And married off!

Uncle Henry let go of my hands. "Fine, then. Let's go back to the house."

"But I haven't explained about Rissy!" I cried. "That awful Mr. Craikey as well as *told* her yesterday what he was going to do with her!"

"Mr. Craikey is a decent man," Uncle Henry said firmly. "He's been our neighbor for years. He does whip his people sometimes, but Rissy's a nice, obedient child. I'm sure she won't have any trouble."

I guessed Uncle Henry had to have it spelled out for him. "He was going to do indecent things to her."

Uncle Henry replied, "I don't know where you got such an idea, but I can assure you it isn't true."

"It is true! He does whatever he wants with his women. If they don't let him do it, he whips them."

My uncle lost patience. "Mary Gillian, this is hardly an appropriate topic for us to discuss. Now let's go back to the house."

"But Rissy—"

"Do you want another switching? If you say one more word, you're getting one."

I followed him silently back to the house and went

straight to my room. I heard Uncle Henry bellowing for Josie to bring him fresh waffles and heat up the potatoes.

I didn't know when I'd ever felt so awful. Rissy was gone, and Mr. Craikey might be doing unspeakable things to her even now. Pa was gone, and I might never see him again.

Don't think about Pa right now, I told myself. Think about how to help Rissy.

I could sneak over to Mr. Craikey's some night and get her to run away with me. Even though she hadn't wanted to go with me before, surely she'd rather do that than have to live with Mr. Craikey. We'd take my flour sack and go West together. We'd find Pa. Or we'd go to Canada. Or we'd find some hidden-away place and live there on our own, forever if we had to.

"Courage and determination," I murmured.

But I knew I was just being rash and foolish again. How would I know what cabin Rissy was in? And what if we got caught? I'd get another hickory switch, but Rissy'd get a cowhide whip. Mr. Craikey might even put chains or an iron collar on her or sell her South.

I needed the Spirit to help me save Rissy. Thank goodness I'd discovered that David was the Spirit! I'd find out how to get to his farm, then tonight, when everyone was asleep, I'd steal a horse from the barn and ride there. I'd tell him about Rissy and he'd go to the Craikeys' and rescue her. I'd have to explain things to Sarah, but—

Sarah. I'd forgotten. David was on his way to New York with Sarah. He couldn't help me.

I heard light footsteps outside my door, followed by some thumps and a scrabbling noise. As I watched, two very squashed waffles slid under the door. A scrap of paper followed. I picked it up and read,

SORRY YOUR IN TRUBLE YOU SURE

CAN YELL

YOUR FREND NEDDY HAYDEN

I ate the waffles quickly and gratefully.

I didn't do my chores that morning, and nobody tried to make me. After I got tired of staying in my room, I left the house and went down to the river. The tree branch over the water wasn't a very comfortable place to sit, considering where Uncle Henry's hickory switch had left a soreness, but I gingerly settled myself onto the branch and tried to think.

After a minute, I decided that thinking was a bad idea. My mind felt like a tired old rag that had been boiled and wrung out too many times. There were holes where all the comforting thoughts and helpful ideas should have been. So instead of thinking, I watched the river flowing and sparkling in the sun.

I stayed there until I ached from being in one position for too long. Then I wandered through the woods for a while, my brain still feeling numb and lifeless. On the way back to the house, I stopped by Clio's cabin. I wanted to get the primer from under Rissy's straw mattress and sneak it back into the house before anybody found it. What if word got to Mr. Craikey that Rissy could read and write?

Clio was asleep, as I'd hoped she would be. But when I took the primer out from under the mattress, I heard her stir.

"Miz Gilly?" she said weakly.

"Can I get you anything?" I asked her, slipping the primer back out of sight. "Some broth or tea, maybe, or something to eat?"

"No'm, I don't need nothin'. I just wanted to say I know you're worried about Rissy."

"Of course I am. Clio, I have to help her."

She propped herself up on her forearms. "No'm. That's what I wanted to tell you. I know you probably got some idea of rescuin' her from Mas' Craikey's, and what I want to say is, don't."

"Don't?"

She shook her head. "Don't be tryin' to help her. You can't do her no good. You'll only make things worse."

"But, Clio, Mr. Craikey's going to—to hurt her! I have to get her away from there!"

"She'll be better off if you leave her alone," Clio repeated firmly, and settled down to sleep again.

I left the cabin angrily. Leave her alone, indeed!

At the house, I thanked Neddy for the waffles.

He looked pleased. "I had to jump on them to make them flat enough to go under the door. It's okay, though—I took off my shoes first."

He looked around to see if anybody was listening. "Did you cry?" he whispered. "Out in the barn with Papa?"

"No."

He nodded. "I *knew* you wouldn't. I always do, but you're braver than me."

Impulsively I bent down and hugged him. If this house caught fire, I thought, he'd be the only person I'd save.

I missed dinner, so by suppertime I was starving. When I went into the dining room, Aunt Laura said, "Mary Gillian, I'm not sure you're ready to act civil at the dining table. Perhaps you'd prefer to fix a plate and eat in your room."

I thought Uncle Henry was the one who was having trouble acting civil, but I did prefer to eat in my room. I filled a plate with fried chicken, mashed potatoes, and turnips, and took it and a glass of water upstairs.

When someone knocked on the door a little while later, I opened it, expecting to see Neddy. It was Aunt Laura.

I started to shut the door, but she caught it. In a low voice, she said, "I must tell you one thing, and I want you to listen: *if you really want to help Rissy, leave her alone.*"

That was exactly what Clio had said! But then, neither she nor Aunt Laura cared about Rissy.

"I know," I said bitterly. "You think it's best if I just leave her alone and let her get accustomed to being mistreated. After all, she's only a slave girl."

Aunt Laura stood there and looked at me, without blinking and without any expression on her face. When she finally spoke, her words were quiet and intense. "You're getting involved in a situation that you know nothing about. I know this is hard for you, Mary Gillian, but you have to accept the fact that *you don't always know what's best*." She let her eyes bore into me for a moment before she turned and left.

Well, I didn't care! It was one thing to allow as how her remedies might be as good as mine—but when it came to Rissy, I did know best. I was Rissy's friend. I cared about her. Aunt Laura and Clio didn't. Besides, Clio wouldn't risk her neck to help anybody, and my aunt didn't believe in rescuing slaves. "They simply couldn't manage on their own," she'd told David in that smug, know-it-all voice of hers.

I was so angry, I threw my pillow at the door. It made a loud thunk, and I didn't know whether I was disappointed or relieved that my aunt and uncle didn't hear it.

I paced the floor for a long time. Once it started getting dark, I looked out the window for Rissy's and my star. I could send Rissy my love on it, as well as Pa.

I scanned the sky closely. If I couldn't see our star from my window, I guessed I could use another one. After all, any of them would—

Suddenly I turned away from the window. How foolish I'd been! Stars couldn't send messages. They sat way up there in the sky, where they weren't even touched by the troubles people on Earth had. They didn't care about pas who went missing or friends who got sold. "Dang-blasted, no-account, good-for-nothing stars," I muttered.

The next day I ate at the table and did my chores, but it was as if my body was doing those things without my mind. I kept thinking about what Mr. Craikey might be doing to Rissy at that very moment. And when I wasn't thinking about that, I was thinking about what Uncle Henry had said. I supposed that deep down I'd always known Pa might be dead or might not send for me. But having to admit it, even to myself, was like sticking a knife in my bosom.

Uncle Henry hadn't gotten the mail on Tuesday, since he'd been busy preparing for Sarah's wedding. When he brought it home Friday afternoon, I didn't have the heart to look at it. He or Aunt Laura would have told me if there was a letter from Pa.

Neddy came into the parlor while I was working my way through the pile of mending. "One day next week, we can go over to the Craikeys' house and visit Rissy," he said. "That is, if Papa lets us and Mr. Craikey doesn't mind."

"We'll see." I knew he was trying to cheer me up. "Thanks, Neddy."

I went to bed early that evening, but I couldn't sleep. Outside, the wind blew and hail rattled against the windows. I hoped Rissy had a dry cabin to sleep in.

What would happen to Rissy? And what would happen to *me* if Pa never sent for me? Would I stay here and mend clothes for the rest of my life? Would I be married off to somebody without having any say in the matter, the way Aunt Laura had been?

If so, maybe I'd end up being like her. After all, from what Miss Bussy had said, Aunt Laura had been a lot like me once. And now she was a stout, unadventurous, humorless old battleax. I surely didn't want to become that way, too.

I tried to picture myself as a grownup woman, pinch-faced and stern like my aunt. I'd have a family and a household to care for, and I'd never get to do anything more exciting than counting the tablecloths in the linen cabinet. Pa and Rissy would be distant memories.

No, I told myself. I wouldn't let that happen. Even if Pa never sent for me, I'd go out West on my own someday. I'd have a little cabin and a garden, and I'd make remedies for folks. I wouldn't get married unless I chose to. I'd make friends with Indians, and I'd catch outlaws, and I'd smoke a pipe like Granny Pea. I'd climb trees and swim rivers and ride a big, fast horse.

I fell asleep wondering whether I'd rather have a black horse or a silver one.

10

THE NEXT THING I KNEW, it was morning and somebody was shaking me.

"Mary Gillian, wake up," Aunt Laura said. "Your uncle and Mr. Craikey are downstairs, waiting to talk to you. Get dressed and come down as quickly as possible."

I blinked sleepily at her. "Why do they want to talk to me?"

"They'll tell you when you get downstairs. Now, hurry! If you aren't down there in five minutes, I'll send them up here."

That got me out of bed and dressed quicker than a lightning flash.

When I was decent, I opened my bedroom door. Mr. Craikey's voice floated up to me from the parlor.

". . . dad-blame little wench had only been at my place for *one day* when she disappeared. And I paid eight hundred dollars for her!"

I caught my breath as I realized what he was saying: there was no need for me to worry about how to rescue Rissy. She'd already escaped on her own.

Uncle Henry and Mr. Craikey stood up when I came into the parlor.

"Gilly, look alive," my uncle said briskly. "We have some serious questions for you."

"For me?"

Mr. Craikey looked down at me sternly. "Your uncle tells me you're a friend of that little girl I bought. You'll save yourself and her both a lot of trouble if you'll tell me where she is."

"What do you mean?" I asked innocently.

"She's gone," Mr. Craikey said. "Her bed was empty this morning, and nobody can find her. It's pretty clear she's run off, the blasted little wench—although why she chose to leave last night, I don't know. You'd think even a slave gal would have more sense than to run off during a hailstorm."

Uncle Henry asked, "Gilly, do you know where Rissy is?"

"No, sir."

"She won't be hurt if she gives herself up this morning," Mr. Craikey said. "I'll take her home real peaceful-like and we'll forget all about it. Why, she'll even be home in time for breakfast. But if she hasn't come to light by dinnertime," he continued, "I'll have to go looking for her with my dogs. And when I find her, I'll whip the Devil out of her—if there's enough left to whip after my hounds have finished with her, that is. So if you know where your little friend is, you'll be doing her a real big favor by telling me."

"I don't know where she is."

"You better think real hard, now," he said, his voice threatening. "Maybe you know something that'll help me. Where did you little girls like to play?"

"We never had time to play. We always had too much work to do."

"You know if she's got any kinfolk?"

"She doesn't. Her ma died and her pa ran off."

Mr. Craikey was getting impatient. I could tell because his face was red and his lips were tight, and he was breathing harder and faster.

Uncle Henry said, "You don't want Mr. Craikey's dogs to get Rissy, do you?"

"No, sir, but I don't know where she is."

"You'd be doing Rissy a favor by helping Mr. Craikey," said Aunt Laura.

But last night, I remembered, she'd told me to leave

Rissy alone if I wanted to help her. It was too puzzling for me to figure out, so I said, "Yes, ma'am, but I don't know where she is."

Mr. Craikey exploded. "Dad-blame it! If you were my brat, I'd get some answers out of you!"

"Easy, Simon," said Uncle Henry quietly.

"Can I go now?" I asked. "I truly don't know where she is."

Nobody answered.

Mr. Craikey squatted down to where his face was level with mine. He gave me what I guessed he thought was a pleasant smile. It had about as much resemblance to a smile as bear grease did to butter.

"Gilly, honey," he asked softly, "is there something you got a hankering for?"

I just stared at him, not understanding. The only things I had a hankering for were Rissy and Pa.

"How about, say, a new dolly or a pretty dress? Or maybe some hair ribbons? *All* little girls like hair ribbons." His voice was silky smooth, mesmerizing. "Maybe some candy. What kind of candy do you like, Gilly? When I was your age, I liked peppermint sticks and bull's-eyes. What do you like?"

I shrugged. What did those things have to do with Rissy?

"I'll tell you what, honey. You help me find your

friend and I'll buy *aaaaany*thing you want—dresses, toys, you name it. Is it a deal?"

That *vermin*! I thought of spitting in his face, but I didn't want him to have anything of mine, not even my spit.

"What will it be, Gilly, honey? A dollhouse? A new jump rope?"

I was shaking with anger. But screaming and swearing hadn't gotten me anywhere with Uncle Henry, and I knew it wouldn't scare Mr. Craikey.

Suddenly I thought of Granny Pea. How would she have handled this?

I looked Mr. Craikey in the eye. "My pa," I said in a tight little voice, "did *not* bring me up to be a liar or a traitor. I do *not* know where Rissy is and I will *not* be bribed. Good *day*, Mr. Craikey."

I tossed my head, turned sharply, and climbed slowly up the steps. I made sure I kept my back straight and my head high, the way Granny Pea would have.

"Well, my word!" I heard Aunt Laura gasp. She didn't sound angry, just astonished.

After I'd shut the door to my room, I sat down on my trundle bed and gave a couple of ragged sobs. Acting dignified when you were scared and furious sure took a lot out of you, especially when you didn't have much practice at it.

The adults were still talking downstairs. I opened the door a crack so I could hear them.

Uncle Henry was saying, ". . . shouldn't have tried to bribe her, Simon. Gilly's not the kind of child you can bribe."

I smiled to myself.

Mr. Craikey snorted. "You people are spoiling that child! Why, if she was mine, I'd thrash her until she *begged* to give me answers." He sighed. "Well, never mind. I'll go talk to Tolliver."

I made a face. Tolliver had helped look for Patsy and the others because he'd been promised a reward if he found them. Old buzzard, I thought. That was what he was: a mean old black, stoop-shouldered, red-eyed buzzard who preyed on the misfortunes of other people.

Somebody knocked on my door and whispered, "Gilly!"

"Neddy?"

His hair was tousled and his shirt was buttoned wrong.

"I heard what you said to Mr. Craikey," he said. "You're the bravest person I know!"

"Thanks. Come on in. Here, let me redo your shirt." I started pulling the buttons out of the wrong holes and putting them through the right ones.

"I'll help you look for Rissy," he said. "I liked her. Carter said she'd bring him and Nancy leftover cake when she could have eaten it herself. And I *don't* like Mr.

Craikey. Every Sunday he tells me how much I've grown, but I can't have grown that much since the Sunday before. Besides, when he smiles, he looks like he's going to eat me."

I told him to look in the outbuildings while I looked in the woods.

"If you find her," I said, "tell her to stay hidden. Say I'll come help her get away before dinner. That's when the grownups are going to start looking for her."

"Where will you take her?"

I hesitated. "I don't know. But I'll think of a place."

At breakfast, my aunt and uncle kept asking me questions about where Rissy might have gone. I said "I don't know" so many times I wondered if I should write it on my forehead. Meanwhile, the clock in the parlor was ticking away the minutes until Mr. Craikey's bloodhounds would go after Rissy.

As we were leaving the dining room, I felt Aunt Laura's hand on my shoulder. Without smiling, she said, "You behaved well this morning with Mr. Craikey. I hope I'm correct in thinking that you may be growing up a bit."

"Yes, ma'am. Thank you."

She looked as if she was going to say something else, but then she just nodded brusquely and walked on.

I hurried out to the woods. The hailstorm had left it uncommonly cool for June, and I was glad I'd put on the warm black shawl Granny Pea had knitted for me. I pulled it tight around me. As I walked along the creek, I hollered, "Rissy! It's me, Gilly! Where are you?" There was no answer except the cawing of the crows and the distant tapping of a woodpecker. Usually that very peacefulness was one of the things I liked best about the woods. That morning, though, I would have given a lot to have it broken by a voice saying, "Gilly, over here! It's me, Rissy."

A few times I heard a rustling sound and stood still, my heart full of hope. But always a rabbit or a pair of squirrels scampered out of the brush and that was all.

Where could Rissy be, except in the woods? Mr. Craikey was right: she couldn't have gone very far in the storm. Maybe she had gotten wet and taken ill, and was too weak to answer my calls. Or maybe David had helpers in his Spirit work, and they had rescued her. But how would they have known she needed rescuing? And how could they have arranged it so quickly?

I covered the whole woods—all the way to the river and clear through to Mr. Craikey's fence. No Rissy. By the time I got back to the farmyard, the sun was high. I was sweating and my stomach was growling.

Neddy was in the back yard. When he saw me, his eyes lit up.

"Gilly, guess what I found!"

My heart jumped. "Rissy?"

"Hmm? Oh, no. But I found a black snake that

stretched halfway across the barn floor! I bet it's ten feet long."

"You were supposed to be looking for Rissy," I said.

"I was, but I didn't find her. Come on, I'll show you the snake!"

The snake truly was a fine one, but I didn't feel as much wonderment as I normally would have. Neddy was disappointed that I didn't praise it more highly. He left to go help Carter gather the eggs, and I looked through the outbuildings myself.

No Rissy.

I went down to the quarters and looked in the cabin where the dance had been held.

Still no Rissy.

I stopped by Clio's cabin. Clio was asleep, so I decided to retrieve Neddy's primer from under Rissy's mattress. If somebody found it and spread the word that Rissy could read, she'd be in more danger than ever.

The primer was gone.

I knelt there on the floor, holding up the thin straw mattress and staring in disbelief. Surely Rissy hadn't been foolish enough to come back and get it herself. But who else would have taken it? And had the person known it was there, or found it by accident?

I felt chilled to the bone. Did somebody know that I'd been teaching Rissy to read?

I went back to the house, more worried than ever.

Josie was carrying a soup tureen across the porch. It was dinnertime.

I ate only one little piece of corn bread and a few spoonfuls of fish chowder.

"Simon will come over with his dogs in a while," Uncle Henry said. He'd just filled his bowl for the second time and put three more pieces of corn bread on his plate. "I hope we can find that little wench before nightfall. If not, we'll have to spend the night out, in case she's waiting until after dark to make a move."

"Maybe the Spirit took her," Neddy said, sounding hopeful.

"Hush your mouth!" Aunt Laura snapped.

"Gilly," said my uncle, "if you want to help Rissy, this is your last chance to speak up."

"Yes, sir, but I don't know where she is."

He sighed. "It's up to you whether you help or not. But you're to stay out of the woods while Simon's dogs are there."

After dinner, Aunt Laura sat me down in the parlor to finish stitching a new shift for Nancy. "Busy hands make time fly," she pronounced.

"It's ugly," I said, holding up the sack-like garment of coarse cotton.

"Nancy won't mind," my aunt replied.

But I remembered how Rissy had loved her new

dresses, and there weren't any pretty hand-me-downs to fit poor little Nancy. She'd have only this shift to wear day after day. So after I'd stitched the seams of her shift, I got Sarah's embroidery box and sewed a red flower on the front. Then I sewed a blue one next to it, and added green leaves. I was determined that Nancy have something pretty! Besides, making the flowers kept me from picturing Rissy getting shot or being mauled by Mr. Craikey's bloodhounds.

Aunt Laura came in while I was finishing the embroidery work. I thought she was going to lecture me on the foolishness of putting flowers on a little slave girl's everyday shift, but she stood there and watched over my shoulder. Then she said, "You know the woods pretty well, don't you?"

I looked up, startled. "Why, yes, ma'am. I go there sometimes."

"Do you know how to get to the river?"

"Yes, ma'am. You just follow the creek."

I was about to ask why she wanted to know, when she said briskly, "Well, you stay out of those woods for the next few days. There'll be patrollers and dogs all over it, looking for that dratted girl. And don't dawdle over that shift. You'll have plenty more things to sew tomorrow. I'll check on your progress after I've taken Clio her boneset tea."

Late that afternoon, while I was hemming Nancy's

shift, I heard the back door slam. I threw down my sewing and ran out into the hallway.

"Uncle Henry! Did you find her?"

He shook his head. "No, we didn't find her. And don't look so relieved, because we'll be going out again tonight. Simon Craikey is determined to find that wench and use her as an example to the rest of his people."

"Wh-what will he do to her?"

My uncle said, "Never you mind."

Aunt Laura came down the steps, her eyebrows raised in a silent question.

"We found nothing," Uncle Henry told her. "We'll go out again tonight after dark. Dang-blast it! I'm starting to wonder if Neddy was right, if the Spirit really does have that girl."

I opened my mouth to say that the Spirit couldn't have Rissy because he was in New York with Sarah. Luckily, I caught myself in time.

Aunt Laura sniffed. "Hmmph! That Spirit should have to pay for all the property he's stolen from honest, hard-working people."

"If he's ever caught," Uncle Henry said grimly, "he'll pay with his life. Now I'm going upstairs to wash up for supper. It'll be on the table soon, I hope."

My aunt nodded and turned to me. "Mary Gillian, you'll have to bring in supper tonight. Josie's still not well enough to put in a full day."

"Me!" I cried, outraged. "If you think—"

"Do as you're told!" Uncle Henry snapped.

"Yes, sir," I muttered. No wonder he'd been so quick to sell Rissy. I could hear him and my aunt now: *We can sell the house girl and use Mary Gillian instead.*

"Put away your sewing and go out to the kitchen," Aunt Laura directed. "Tolliver will give you instructions. He's expecting you. I'll set the table myself. Hurry now! And wipe that sullen look off your face."

I put Nancy's shift, the needles, and the pins into the sewing basket, and returned the embroidery things to Sarah's box. But I didn't stop frowning. Nobody could make me smile unless they stuck their fingers in the corners of my mouth and pulled my lips up.

I stomped out to the kitchen, angry and resentful. I was expected not only to do Rissy's work but also to take orders from that old buzzard Tolliver, who was willing to help Mr. Craikey look for her.

Tolliver was bending over several three-legged pots that were sitting above coals on the stone floor in front of the fireplace.

I said coldly, "Aunt Laura said I have to serve supper."

He looked at me briefly, then pulled a couple of the pots off the coals.

"Them peas and turnips needs to cool a spell," he said, and stood up. "Meanwhile, we gots to have us a talk."

"But I know how to carry bowls of food! Why do we—"

"Sit down and quit your jabberin'. This be important."

I sat on the chair. Tolliver pulled up a wooden stool and sat facing me.

"Miz Hayden say you know them woods. That be true?"

"Yes. But if you think I'm going to help Mr. Craikey find Rissy—"

"That ain't what I be thinkin'! Don't try to guess my thoughts, gal. Now, does you know how to get to the riverbank? There by that leanin' tree where the little stream come out?"

"Yes, but—"

"You think you able to get there at night, without no lantern?"

"I'm sure I could. My pa says I've got eyes like a cat at night."

Tolliver crossed his arms and looked at me critically. "Miz Hayden think you got it in you to be brave and dependable if you has a mind to be."

"She does?"

"Yes'm. And tonight you better have a mind to be. You better not do no braggin' and boastin' afterward, neither."

I couldn't help giggling. "But all I'm going to do is carry food to the dining room."

"Well, that's all you needs to worry about right now, anyways. I ain't gonna tell you no more. You go serves supper and don't let on that we had this talk. Hear?"

"Y-yes."

Tolliver put the peas and mashed turnips into Aunt Laura's china serving dishes. He scowled at me as he handed me the bowl of peas. I scowled back.

When Neddy saw me carrying the bowl into the dining room, he whispered, "Look, Papa! Gilly's serving dinner. Is she one of our people now?"

"No, son, she's just helping out until Clio gets well," Uncle Henry said.

"You won't sell her, will you, Papa? Like you did Rissy?"

"Neddy, hush," Aunt Laura said. "Don't be ridiculous."

I made several more trips, to bring in the bowl of turnips, a platter of pork chops, and a tray holding the silver gravy boat, a dish of butter, and a loaf of bread. Then I took my place at the table, but I only picked at my food. The idea of Rissy being hunted down by bloodhounds made my throat close up.

"We'll go back out tonight about ten o'clock," Uncle Henry told Aunt Laura. "Simon wants to take the dogs through the woods again. We'll go down to the riverbank, too."

He shoveled mashed turnips into his mouth. The thought of chasing an innocent young girl with shotguns and a pack of killer dogs didn't harm *his* appetite any.

He took a long drink of water, then turned back to Aunt Laura.

"We'll also follow up that lead you gave us," he said, "about the girl maybe having an aunt down near Culpeper."

I gasped. "Rissy never—"

"Get your elbows off the table!" my aunt snapped at me. "How many times do I have to tell you? And don't chew with your mouth open, either."

"But I wasn't—"

Uncle Henry said, "Don't talk back, Gilly."

"Yes, sir," I muttered.

I sawed my pork chop angrily, wishing it was my aunt's neck. My elbows had *not* been on the table, and I *never* chewed with my mouth open!

Aunt Laura said to Uncle Henry, "Yes, Clio thought Rissy once mentioned an aunt who's a field hand in those parts. It might be worth your sending some patrollers that way."

This time I didn't say anything, but I thought plenty. Dang-blast my aunt, trying to help find Rissy! And why hadn't Rissy ever told me about having an aunt near Culpeper?

After we'd finished our meal, Aunt Laura looked at me and said, "We're ready for dessert now."

"Ma'am?" I looked at her. She motioned toward the kitchen with her head, and I realized she meant for me to go fetch the rhubarb pie I'd seen cooling on the kitchen table.

I glowered as I went out the door. At home we ate in front of the fireplace and served ourselves. That made more sense than having one person, namely me, put on her shawl and trot back and forth to the kitchen while everybody else stayed comfortable.

I fetched the pie and Aunt Laura cut it. From under the flaky, golden-brown crust flowed thick pink juice and sweetened hunks of pale red rhubarb. But because that worry worm was twisting around inside me, I ended up slipping most of my slice onto Neddy's plate.

Uncle Henry had two pieces of pie, and he didn't leave a smidgen.

When he'd finished, Aunt Laura said, "Mary Gillian, please take the leftover food and the dishes out to the kitchen. As a matter of fact, I shall take some myself. I need to talk to Tolliver about tomorrow's menu."

Once we'd left the porch, she whispered, "I'm sorry for accusing you of ill manners at the table. You'll soon understand why I had to do it."

I was so startled I stopped and stared at her. Aunt Laura was apologizing to *me* for something? And what did she mean, that I'd soon understand?

She glanced at me over her shoulder and, in a low voice, said, "Come along! There's no time to waste."

My heart pounded with excitement as I followed her down the stone path to the kitchen.

11

TOLLIVER WAS SITTING ON A STOOL in the kitchen, eating his own meal.

"Set the dishes on the table," my aunt told me. She set down her own pile of plates and turned to Tolliver. "Is everything ready?"

"Yes'm."

Aunt Laura nodded. "Henry and Simon are going out at ten. There should be time."

She looked at me. "I have to go back to the house now. I'll tell your uncle and Neddy that you're helping Tolliver clean the kitchen."

"But what *will* I be doing?" I asked, exasperated. "What's happening, anyway?"

"You'll find out shortly," my aunt said. "Do what Tolliver tells you."

After she'd gone, Tolliver said, "Come on, li'l gal, you follow me upstairs. And don't go fallin' down them steps and breakin' your neck, neither, 'cause we ain't got no time for that."

I put my shawl on the table and started to pick up a lantern. Tolliver shook his head.

"Don't you be bringin' no light! You say your eyes be like a cat's, remember?"

Mystified, I followed him up the curving stone steps. Halfway up, I stopped and shivered. Josie thought there was a ghost up there, and I *had* seen that white curtain move one night for no reason.

"Come on, gal, what you stoppin' for?"

"Nothing," I replied. I'd rather be gotten by a ghost than admit my fears to Tolliver.

We started across the herb room. Something brushed my head, and I almost screamed before I realized it was a drying bunch of herbs hanging from the rafters. My eyes were getting used to the darkness, though. I could make out the furniture and baskets. But why were we up here? What did this have to do with my serving dinner?

Tolliver didn't stop until he got to the door of the storeroom. Then he took a key out of his pocket and turned to me. "Now, listen, gal. We's trustin' you. If you go around talkin' about this, you gonna get people hurt bad. You understand?"

I didn't, but I said yes.

"Okay, then," he said, and turned the key in the lock.

"You gals come on out now," he said softly into the storeroom. "It's gettin' on time to go. Step out here, Carrie Belle and Rissy."

"Rissy?"

"Yes'm," replied the person who was walking out of the storeroom. Even in the darkness, I saw her grinning. "It's me, Gilly. You surprised?"

Surprised? Flabbergasted was what I was. I stammered, "Wh-what are you doing here?"

"Remember what Mas' Thurmond said about the underground railroad?" she replied. "Well, this here's a station on it. Miz Hayden and Tolliver are the stationmasters. Clio's a conductor. That's why she went out during the night that time we thought she had a beau. But now she's sick, so *you* gotta be the conductor and get us down to the river to meet the boat that'll take us over to Maryland."

My thoughts tumbled around so madly I couldn't grasp them. The storeroom was a hiding place for runaway slaves? Aunt Laura and Tolliver were stationmasters? Quiet, obedient Clio was a conductor?

No wonder Aunt Laura didn't want people coming up to the herb room!

"This is Carrie Belle," Rissy said, gesturing toward the tall young woman who had stepped out of the storeroom after her. "She came from Charlottesville a coupla weeks ago. She took sick while she was runnin' away, and Doc Granger brought her here so Miz Hayden could take care of her."

Dr. Granger! *A large package of motherwort . . . not as strong as usual . . .*

"Tolliver, is that what the notes are about?" I cried. "The ones Dr. Granger writes to Aunt Laura about delivering herbs?"

"I ain't sayin'," he said. "You got no business readin' them notes, anyways. And you, Rissy gal, don't you be namin' names like that. You know what Miz Hayden say—it be safer if nobody knows who else helps in this here operation."

I put in, "I already know David Thurmond is helping. I figured it out for myself. He's the Spirit!"

Rissy giggled. "No, he ain't. We got it all wrong, Gilly. Mas' Thurmond ain't the Spirit. Miz Hayden's the Spirit."

"Ain't no one person the Spirit," Tolliver grumbled. "It be too much work for one person. Mas' Thurmond, though, he ain't got no part in the underground railroad at all, not as far as I knows."

I felt dizzy. Handsome, dashing David wasn't the Spirit, after all. The Spirit was made up of stodgy Aunt

Laura, grouchy Tolliver, dutiful Clio, and easygoing Dr. Granger. And, as of tonight, *me*—rash, boasting Gilly Bucket.

I swallowed nervously.

Tolliver said, "Now it's time you quit your jawin' and do some listenin'. You gots to meet a boat on the river at ten-thirty."

"But Uncle Henry and Mr. Craikey are going out with the dogs at ten," I told him. "They'll be in the woods."

"Then you gots to be through them woods and down to the river by then," Tolliver retorted. "That boat gonna slide up alongside the bank to where that big ol' tree leans out over the water. You gots to watch and listen close, 'cause it's gonna slip along quiet as a fish. It can't be waitin' for you, neither. There may be other passengers needin' to get to safety."

"Where will the boat take us?" Carrie Belle asked.

"That I don't know, and Clio and Miz Hayden don't know, neither. We don't know nothin', not even who the boatman be. This way even if we gets caught, we can't tell nobody nothin', not even if they threatens to hang us."

Hang Aunt *Laura*? Surely Uncle Henry wouldn't let that happen. Or would he? He had said more than once that the Spirit should be hanged. Would he still think so if he knew it was Aunt Laura?

Tolliver continued, "When you gets to the river, you hide on the banks until you sees that boat slidin' along toward you. Then you sing the first bar of that tune, 'Wade in the Water.' You know that one, gal?"

Rissy nodded.

"Sing it real low and soft. That be the code to tell the boatman you's there. When the boat comes up, you jump in quick-like. Don't be trippin' and splashin' and such. And you, Miz Gilly, you gotta sneak back through the woods afterward and get home without runnin' into Mas' Craikey and his men."

"I've heard that Mas' Craikey has the best bloodhounds in all of Virginny," Carrie Belle said in a tight, scared voice.

Tolliver said, "I's gonna give you pepper to rub on your feet to confuse them dogs. And recollect what Miz Hayden taught you about wadin' in the creek. Even the best bloodhounds in Virginny can't smell you when you's in the creek."

I understood now why Tolliver had taken food from the icehouse and why he had sneaked over here in the night. But a couple of things were still puzzling. "Tolliver," I said, "if you're part of the Spirit, how come you helped Mr. Craikey look for Patsy and the others? And if Aunt Laura's part of the Spirit, how come she told Uncle Henry that Rissy has kinfolk near Culpeper?"

"Me?" Rissy said. "I haven't got kinfolk near Culpeper."

"Use your brains, Miz Gilly!" Tolliver scoffed. "Miz Hayden and me, we sets them men off in the wrong directions. Why, when Patsy and them left, I had 'em goin' every which way 'cept the right one! Now I gotta go downstairs and fix your provisions. You do all your talkin' here, 'cause once you gets outside, your lives gonna depend on you bein' quiet as li'l mice."

After he'd gone downstairs, I asked, "Rissy, did Mr. Craikey hurt you? How did you get away? How did you know to come here?"

She replied, "He never touched me 'cause Miz Craikey was watchin' the whole time. She knew he was makin' sheep's eyes at me, and she slapped me every chance she got. Said I was uppity and stupid. Hmmph! As for how I got here, Miz Hayden had it figured out before I even knew I was goin' to Mas' Craikey's. The mornin' he came for me, I went to get my things from the cabin, and Clio told me to leave Mas' Craikey's at midnight. She said to hide in the bushes till I was sure it was safe, then follow the road back here, where Tolliver'd meet me. I wanted to be spirited away right then, but she said I had to go to Mas' Craikey's first so he wouldn't guess who was helpin' me. Anyway, I was lucky, 'cause the weather was so purely awful last night nobody saw me leave. I didn't even mind the hail peltin' me, I was so glad to get shut of Mas' Craikey's. And Tolliver, he said the weather wasn't the only reason I was lucky. He said the boat was supposed to come on June first to pick up Carrie Belle and not come again until the next new moon. I woulda had to spend nearly a whole month in that storeroom." She shuddered. "But the boat waited until tonight, June fourth, 'cause the underground railroad was bringin' another passenger for it."

A change from June first to June fourth, I thought. Why did that seem familiar?

Change the proportions on that motherwort tea, from six and one to six and four, Dr. Granger had told my aunt after Sarah's wedding.

June was the sixth month of the year!

"I shouldn't complain about that storeroom, though," Rissy said. "It's a good hidin' place. Miz Hayden showed me how if you hear the slave-catchers comin', you can pry up a hunk of the floorboards and get underneath. Then you pull it over you and lie flat between it and the kitchen ceilin' till it's safe to come out. She said Tolliver'd rattle the pots and pans real loud downstairs so nobody'd hear anything."

"Sometimes Miz Hayden would leave the storeroom door unlocked at night," Carrie Belle told me. "That way I could come out here into the herb room and get me some exercise. She made me promise not to look out of them windows, in case anybody was watchin', but sometimes I'd peek out anyway. Two weeks is a mighty long time not to see the outside world."

That was why I'd seen one of the curtains move, my first night at Glencaren! A shut-in slave hadn't been able to resist looking out the window.

"Miz Hayden kept me plenty busy for them two weeks, though," Carrie Belle continued. "She taught me my alphabet, and even had me readin' a few words."

"She was pleased I already knew my letters," Rissy added. "I had her go get that primer from under my mattress so I could keep on with my lessons. She guessed it was you who'd taught me, Gilly! She said that was one reason she chose you to help us tonight."

Tolliver was coming back up the stairs.

"I have maps and a knife and money you can have," I told Rissy and Carrie Belle.

"Miz Hayden already gave us them things," Carrie Belle drawled. "She taught us all about the North Star and about moss growin' on the north side of trees, and about how to walk quiet and hide in the woods."

"Oh," I said meekly.

"We sure was wrong about Miz Hayden," Rissy said, as though she were reading my thoughts.

I nodded. I was feeling almighty humble, and it wasn't a comfortable feeling.

"You all come downstairs to the kitchen now," Tolliver said.

There he gave Rissy and Carrie Belle their bag of provisions. Then he rubbed soot from the fireplace on my face so it would be less visible in the dark.

"Can I wear britches, too?" I asked eagerly, seeing what the other two were wearing.

Tolliver shook his head. "What if Mas' Craikey catches you on the way home? You gotta act like you's just out lookin' for Rissy, wearin' your everyday clothes. Remember to wash that soot off, too, before you leaves the river. And you come back here to the kitchen, not to the big house. If Mas' Henry come home early, you don't want him to see you comin' in."

"Now, no more talkin'!" he cautioned as he led us to the door. "Stay hid and quiet, and use your common sense."

I thought he looked extra hard at me when he said that, but I wasn't sure.

"Bye, Tolliver," Rissy whispered. "Thanks for all you did!"

"Take care of you'self, gal," he said gruffly. "You, too, Carrie Belle."

It was cool out, and I was glad I had my shawl. The three of us crept through the trees around the clearing, behind the outbuildings and cabins. Clio's cabin was dark, but lanterns still glowed in some of the others. I heard Nancy crying and Dilsey singing her a lullaby.

Once we got to the woods, it was as dark as the inside of a bear. There was a thumbnail of a moon, not enough to see by. Without any moonlight, it was hard to walk— but it would also be hard for Mr. Craikey and his men to see us.

I led Rissy and Carrie Belle to the creek bank. It was steep on our side and we'd have to be careful, but following it was the best way to get to the river.

Behind me, the other two were quiet and sure-footed. Aunt Laura had taught them well, I thought. My job might not be so hard, after all.

As we walked, I mused on my aunt. How did she manage to show the world a Laura Hayden that was so different from the true one? And to keep her secret from Uncle Henry day after day? Until tonight I'd figured that, even though she and Uncle Henry hadn't married for love, they'd been a perfect match—both of them stodgy and close-minded, like two oxen hitched together. But they were so different that Aunt Laura couldn't even share her real life with Uncle Henry! I supposed her being married to him made her work easier, since nobody would suspect Henry Hayden's wife of spiriting away the slaves. Still, how lonely she must be.

Sarah would never know that kind of loneliness, I

thought. Even if David *were* the Spirit and she wasn't daring enough to help him, they'd always know what was in each other's hearts and trust each other.

I was thinking so hard I jumped when Rissy put a hand on my shoulder. "Dogs!" she whispered.

I stopped and listened. Faintly I heard the baying of bloodhounds. The sound got louder, until it seemed to fill my head.

Mr. Craikey and the others had come out early!

My heart was pounding as I motioned for Rissy and Carrie Belle to follow me down the creek bank. We clutched weeds and roots as we went, until we reached the creek itself. We crouched down and stayed still until the baying of the dogs had passed.

"We'd better walk in the creek," I whispered to the other two.

I stood up and carefully led them down the middle of the creek. It was rough going. We took each step cautiously, holding our arms out on both sides to keep our balance.

Splash!

I looked back. Rissy was on her hands and knees in the creek.

"Are you okay?" I whispered.

Her only reply was a little moan.

"She done hurt herself!" Carrie Belle whispered.

Together we helped Rissy to her feet.

She whispered, "I just cut my hand and scraped up my knees. You think them men of Mas' Craikey's heard me?"

"No, they're too far away," I replied. "Can you walk?"

She nodded. But I could feel how hard she was trembling, and when she tried to take a step forward she nearly fell.

"Guess I bruised my left shinbone, too," she admitted. "It hit on a big old rock."

Carrie Belle and I got on either side and put our arms around her to help her walk. It was awkward and slow going. I had to fight down the panic that was rising in me. How long would the boatman wait for us? What if he decided we weren't coming and left before we got there?

If that happened, I realized, I'd have to get Carrie Belle and Rissy safely back to the herb room. And they'd have to hide in that little hole for another month.

"Gilly," whispered Rissy, "maybe you oughtta run on ahead and tell the boatman we're comin'. We can wait here for you."

I thought it over quickly. "No, I might have trouble finding you again. We'd better stay together."

We inched forward. I felt as if I was in one of those nightmares I sometimes had—the ones where huge, angry wild animals were chasing me and I couldn't run.

Frantically Rissy whispered, "I'm slowin' you all down too much!"

"Don't worry." I tried to sound confident. "We'll make it."

At last we saw the clearing up ahead. We felt the creek get wider and deeper as it opened out into the dark, quiet Potomac River.

"Where's the boat?" Carrie Belle whispered.

At first I didn't see it, and I wanted to fall down and sob with fear and tiredness. But then I remembered what Tolliver had said: it would slide up quietly alongside the bank. It would be hard to see and to hear, for us as well as for Mr. Craikey and the men.

I strained my eyes to see into the darkness along the riverbank. "There it is!" I pointed, and grinned with relief.

But the boat wasn't moving.

"Is there anybody in it?" Rissy asked.

Then we heard dogs' baying and men's voices. Torchlights shone through the woods, and they were moving swiftly toward the riverbank. The patrollers were getting closer! No wonder that boat was so still, I thought. The boatman had seen them coming.

I looked around wildly. The only place we could hide was the river. There was a big fallen tree branch a few yards farther out. Its ends were buried in the river soil and its middle part sat a few inches above the water.

"Come on!" I whispered, tying my shawl around my waist.

Carrie Belle and I supported Rissy, and we waded out until the cold water was around our knees, then up to our chests. We went on, shivering and slipping in the mud, until we reached the branch. I showed the other two what we were going to do: get down in the river as low as we could behind that fallen branch, keeping only our noses and eyes above the water. To keep from floating away, we'd cling to twigs that stuck out of the branch under the water.

The patrollers and dogs got closer. The dogs were quiet now, sniffing around the riverbank. We heard the patrollers talking. ". . . may have come to the river and met a boat," one of them was saying, "or ventured out into the water. I've heard of slaves so stupid they'd try to make it across the river, even though they didn't know how to swim."

I thought angrily, those slaves weren't stupid—they were desperate.

"Let's have a look around while we're here," another said. "See anything in the water?"

I ducked my head under the water, and felt ripples as Rissy and Carrie Belle did the same. How long could we hold our breaths? I wondered. How long would we have to? And was my bright red hair floating on the surface? I held it down with one hand while I clung to the twig with the other one.

I counted to sixty and quietly raised my head out of the water.

"I don't see nothing," one of the men was saying. They weren't looking toward us anymore, so I tugged gently on Rissy's hair to let her know that she and Carrie Belle, on the other side of her, could raise their eyes and noses, too.

"No use staying here," the first man said. "Let's go back through the woods. Maybe Simon's found something. Henry Hayden's setting off toward Culpeper. He heard the gal had kinfolk there."

Yes, I thought, he'd heard it from my aunt Laura, who cared enough about the slaves to trick her own husband.

After the men and dogs had turned and left, we waded back up to the riverbank. The boat slid toward us.

"You have to sing to the boatman," I whispered to Rissy.

Softly she sang, "Waaade in the waaa-ter. Wade in the *wa*ter, children."

Just as softly, a man's voice came from the boat. "Waaade in the waa-ter. God's a-gonna trouble the water."

"It's him!" Carrie Belle whispered, clasping her hands. "Hallelujah, and thanks be to the Lord Almighty!"

Rissy and I hugged each other. My tears and hers got all mixed together on our cheeks.

"I'm going to miss you so much!" I whispered.

"I'm gonna miss you just as much, 'cause you're my best friend."

I said, "We'll be best friends for life, no matter how far apart we are."

I heard the boatman sing softly, "Waaade in the water, children!"

I knew that meant he wanted us to hurry.

"I'll wade out with you," I said.

Rissy shook her head. "It's best if you don't see the boatman or any of them other passengers. Remember what Tolliver said: what you don't know, you can't tell."

We hugged again.

I hugged Carrie Belle, too, and said, "Take care of yourself. You'll soon be safe in Canada."

"Yes'm, Miz Gilly, thanks to you and them other Spirit people."

She helped Rissy out to the boat. I saw the boatman steady them as they got in and sat down among the other dark, silent human shapes. Then the boat pulled away, across the river. I soon lost sight of it in the darkness.

I rubbed my face on my black shawl in case the river water hadn't washed all the soot off me. Then I turned to start back home, relieved and sad at the same time. I was also tuckered out, and I didn't feel well. I was as wet as a tadpole and shivering in my soaked dress. The wet shawl around my waist seemed to pull me down to the ground. My skin felt tender, as though Uncle Henry's switch had landed all over me instead of just on my backside. My joints ached, and I had a slight headache.

When I got home, I figured, I'd dry off by the kitchen fire and then sleep for hours and hours. Or maybe I'd ask Aunt Laura to make me a cup of peppermint tea, and we'd sit in the parlor while she told me all about the Spirit and the underground railroad. If Uncle Henry was on his way to Culpeper, we'd be able to talk for a good, long spell.

Suddenly I heard voices ahead of me.

"We went down to the river," a man was saying. "The dogs sniffed all around, but didn't find anything."

Then Simon Craikey's voice said, "You take the dogs and go up to the main road. I'll go down to the river myself and have a look. A boat might have been there and stayed hidden until you left. If so, it'll be out on the river now. If it's still close enough, I can shoot holes in it. If it's too far out on the water, we'll know to go search on the Maryland side."

My heart thudded so hard I was surprised they didn't hear it. Mr. Craikey was exactly right about where that boat would be. I had to keep him away from the river!

I tried to think quickly. My mind felt dull and worn out, but I had an idea.

As soon as the other men left, I walked out right in front of Simon Craikey. He held up his lantern and I took a step back so he couldn't see that I was wet and shaking.

"Why, it's Henry Hayden's little orphan gal!" he exclaimed.

"I'm not an—" I started. But that wasn't important now.

Mr. Craikey chuckled. "Does your uncle know you're out here?"

I decided to act dignified, as I had that morning. "My uncle is very busy. I don't always disturb him by telling him where I'm going."

"And where *are* you going, missy? Or won't you tell old Simon?"

"I'm just going for a walk." I shrugged. I deliberately swallowed hard and turned my head, as if I was hiding something.

"A walk? At this time of night?" Mr. Craikey laughed outright. "Ain't such a good idea, going for a walk in the woods at night when there's patrollers and bloodhounds out! You sure you're not, say, going to the aid of a—uh, *friend in need?*"

"I—I don't know what you mean," I said, trying to sound nervous. "I'm heading home. Good night, now."

I started off through the bushes, away from the river. Then I stood still and listened.

Just as I'd hoped, Mr. Craikey was following me, thinking I was going to Rissy's hiding place. I could hear twigs snapping and branches rustling as he walked.

I led him around in the woods, taking him farther and farther away from the river. At last I decided I'd led him far enough away. I was exhausted and wanted to go home. But I couldn't have Mr. Craikey following me home, or he might figure out that I'd been deliberately leading him away from Rissy. I didn't want him to catch up with me, either. I didn't relish having him beat me to try to get information.

I had to think of a way to lose him in the woods.

Maybe, I thought, he wasn't familiar enough with the woods to know about the steep creek bank. Even though he lived next door, the woods were on Uncle Henry's land.

I headed toward the creek bank, stopping every once in a while to make sure Mr. Craikey was still following me. When I got to the bank, I scooted down it on my backside, hanging on to bushes and twigs along the way. It was rough and bumpy, but I got down in one piece. Then I waded through the creek and climbed easily up the low bank on the other side.

I headed for home. Mr. Craikey, I figured, would stop at the steep bank and lose sight of me while he tried to figure out how to get down it. By the time he'd inched his way down, I'd be drying off by the kitchen fire!

Now that I was safe, the weakness and achiness hit me worse than ever. My head pounded, my skin hurt, and I groaned with the chills that ran through me.

I'm sick, I realized. The thought surprised me. After all, I was as strong as an ox. I *never* got sick.

But it was all I could do to drag myself to the kitchen and open the door.

"Miz Gilly?" Tolliver jumped up from his stool by the fireplace and ran toward me.

"They're safe," I murmured. "The boat came, and they're safe."

Everything began to turn black.

I felt Tolliver grab me just before I hit the floor.

12

AFTER THAT, I didn't know much of anything for a long time. When I was conscious, which wasn't very often, I felt hot and smothered and scratchy, and everything hurt. My eyes hurt, my throat hurt, and my chest hurt. Aunt Laura would spoon nasty-tasting tea and medicine into my mouth. Sometimes I tried to spit them out, and she held my nose to make me swallow them.

I dreamed a lot about Pa. In the good dreams, he and I were back home, walking in the woods or having dinner in front of the fire in our cabin. Often, he played his fiddle. Sometimes Ma would be with us, too. Once I dreamed she was running across a cloud to meet me.

In the bad dreams, Pa'd be in a boiling-hot river, or he'd be in a wildfire and coughing from the smoke, or his chest would be crushed by falling rocks. He'd yell for help. The noise would wake me up, and I'd have the feeling that maybe *I'd* been the one yelling.

Usually when I woke up, Aunt Laura would be sitting beside me. Sometimes it was Clio, but almost always it was Aunt Laura.

Several times Dr. Granger came. Once I heard Uncle Henry ask him if there wasn't something more that could be done, but I didn't know what he meant. I heard Neddy crying, and I wondered what he was so sad about.

Then one day when I woke up, I felt cooler and my chest didn't hurt as much. My eyes and throat no longer felt as if somebody had taken a scrub brush and lye soap to them. For a minute I thought I had died. Then I realized I couldn't have died, because instead of seeing Ma, I saw Rufus Peacock looking down at me—and I knew for sure that Rufus Peacock was no angel.

"*Rufus Peacock!*" I hollered, sitting bolt upright in the big featherbed.

"Lie down, Mary Gillian," Aunt Laura said. "You're very weak."

"But it's *Rufus Peacock!*"

"That's right, Gilly, old Rufus in the flesh!" he said, grinning down at me from behind his bushy black whiskers. "We was starting to think you was a gone coon."

"Where's Pa?"

"Lie *down*, Mary Gillian. Mr. Peacock, please don't get

215

her wrought up. She's still very weak from the influenza and—"

"Rufus, where *is* he? Where's Pa? Is he okay?"

"He's out in Kansas Territory, and he's okay."

My throat tightened up, and I had to whisper the next question.

"Does he want me?"

"Does he *want* you?" Rufus said. "Does he *want* you? Does a fish want water? Does a flower want sunshine? Does a—"

Aunt Laura cleared her throat. "Mr. Peacock, I believe a yes or no will suffice."

"Well then, *yes*, dad-blame it all, of course he wants you! He sent me to fetch you, although he didn't know you'd be clear out here in Virginny."

"But why hasn't he written to me?"

Rufus said, "He did write you, a couple of months ago. He told you how we'd been looking for gold up in the mountains, out of touch with all humanity, and were just getting back to civilization, where he could get a letter mailed. He made it a long letter, too, told you all about—uh, lots of things."

Aunt Laura put in quietly, "I'll go downstairs and let you folks talk. Don't let her get overly tired, Mr. Peacock." Then she slipped out of the room.

"How come I never got Pa's letter?" I asked.

" 'Cause them dad-blamed polecats you stayed with, them Cadwalladers, never sent it on to you. They never sent your letters on to him, neither."

I gasped. "Why not?"

"They thought you'd be better off staying here with your ma's kinfolk instead of going back to your pa. Now, don't get all riled up! Your aunt'll have my hide if I get you riled. Anyways, I got to Prairie Flower, thinking I'd visit my poor dear ma, God rest her soul, and found out about her untimely demise. Your pa was counting on me to fetch you, but I had to threaten to beat the—well, the you-know-what out of them Cadwalladers before they'd tell me where you were."

"I wish you *had* beaten the you-know-what out of them," I told him, remembering how desperately I'd waited to hear from Pa all those weeks.

Rufus said slowly, "You know, I think maybe we ought to tell your pa those letters got lost and not say anything about the Cadwalladers. He might get to thinking maybe they were right in saying you'd be better off here than with him. He felt real bad about what happened, you know."

"You mean about his money being stolen? Or—or *was* it stolen?"

Rufus thought. "In a manner of speaking, it was stolen. See, there was this feller who showed up at the blacksmith shop one day and offered your pa a whole big sum of money to stay late and fix a busted wagon wheel. He said he had to get to St. Louis to sell a load of hard cider and swore that on his way home, when he had the cider money in his pocket, he'd stop and pay your pa in cash. Well, you know how trusting your pa is. He agreed and stayed to fix the wagon wheel. He was so excited about all the money he was getting, he went down to the gambling hall afterward. Pretty soon, he'd gambled away all that money and then some. That was bad enough, but that gol-durned sneaking lickfinger of a cider-selling scalawag absquatulated with the money he owed your pa!"

"Ab—did what with it?"

"Made off with it when it rightly belonged to somebody else."

"Oh. So Pa *did* have to sell his shop to pay his gambling debts."

"I'm afraid so." Rufus sighed. "Gilly, your pa's no saint, and there's no use pretending he is. Still, he's a good man and I think he's learned his lesson now."

I nodded slowly. I was disappointed that Pa had gambled recklessly, but that cider man shouldn't have run off with the money. Besides, Pa *was* a good man and a good pa to me. And we loved each other.

Rufus continued. "That's why your pa doesn't want to go back to Prairie Flower. He wants to start over in a new place so he can get his self-respect back."

"You mean we're not going back to Prairie Flower? Where will we live?"

"Out in Kansas Territory. Your pa's buying the land right now. He took a fancy to it on our way out West, and decided to buy it with some of the gold he found."

"He found gold? Truly?"

"Not as much as I did," Rufus said, "but enough to get the land and some new blacksmith tools. He plans to do repairs for people heading West. And Miz—"

He stopped, looking uncomfortable.

"Miz who?" I asked.

Aunt Laura came into the room. "Mr. Peacock, I'm afraid you'll have to let Mary Gillian rest now. You can talk again later."

"But Rufus is telling me something important!"

"No, Gilly, your aunt's right," Rufus said quickly. "You need to rest."

He nodded to Aunt Laura, and clattered downstairs in his boots.

What was he going to tell me? I wondered. Something about a Miz somebody. Whatever it was, he'd seemed glad Aunt Laura had interrupted.

I went to sleep and dreamed that Pa and I were walking hand in hand beside a cool blue stream. Birds sang, flowers bloomed, and a rainbow arched above us.

When I woke up, I knew I was getting well because I was very, very hungry. The smell of supper drifted up to me along with voices and the clinking of knives and forks on china. I was afraid I'd been forgotten, but finally Neddy came in carrying a tray.

"It's about time," I grumbled, sitting up against the bed pillows. "My stomach thinks my throat's been cut."

"There's not much here," Neddy warned me. He put the tray on my lap and sat down on the edge of the bed.

"Toast and chamomile tea!" I yowled. "But you had fried chicken! I smelled it."

"We had sweet potatoes and stewed greens, too. And chocolate cake for dessert!"

"Chamomile tea tastes like rot," I muttered, glaring at it.

"Mama says you have to drink it."

"Tell her spicebush tea is—" I caught myself. I wasn't going to be bossy to Aunt Laura anymore, ever. Not after finding out about the hidden part of her life.

"Never mind." I sighed. "If your ma thinks chamomile tea's better, I'll drink it."

I took a few sips, then plunked down my teacup and raised my hand to my chest. "Where's my pendant? My forget-me-not?"

Neddy looked around the room.

"It's hanging on the hook with your dress. Do you want me to fetch it for you?"

"No, that's okay. I just wanted to make sure it's safe."

For a second, I thought maybe I'd lost it that night in the woods.

That night. The woods. Rissy.

"Neddy, did Mr. Craikey ever find Rissy?"

"Nope. He and Papa aren't friends anymore, either! He said Papa should give him back the money he spent buying Rissy 'cause he'd gotten the short end of the stick, what with her running off so soon. But Papa said the sale had been fair and legal and that it was Mr. Craikey's own fault if he mistreated his people so badly that a girl ran off the day after he bought her."

"Really?" My respect for Uncle Henry went up a little.

Neddy said, "Guess what, Gilly. Uncle Rufus eats his food with a *knife*!"

"Uncle Rufus?"

"Um-hmm. He said I can call him that. He thinks it has a nice ring to it." Neddy sighed blissfully. "I want to be just like him when I grow up."

I giggled. I could imagine what Aunt Laura would have to say about that.

Later, my aunt came in to help me wash my face, put on a clean nightgown, and do other bodily chores I needed help with. As she was tucking a fresh quilt around me, I told her about Pa finding gold and buying land in Kansas Territory.

"I'm happy for you both," she said. From the way she smiled, I knew she meant it.

"Have you heard from Rissy?" I asked. "Neddy said Mr. Craikey never found her."

My aunt replied, "Rissy and a woman named Carrie Belle left this area over a week ago. They are presumed to be on the underground railroad to Canada."

I sighed with relief. "Aunt Laura, I know about you being the Sp—"

"Quiet!" she said sharply. In a whisper she added, "Whatever you learned that night, you must never say aloud. Now go to sleep."

She took the candle and walked briskly out of the room.

When I woke up in the morning, I got another cup of chamomile tea, but I also got a hotcake and an egg. Best of all, Aunt Laura let Rufus Peacock come talk to me.

"Rufus, what were you starting to say yesterday? It was about a Miz somebody."

"Oh—why, I've plumb forgotten now. Guess it wasn't important. Let me tell you about Kansas Territory."

I thought he'd replied a little too quickly to be convincing, but I did want to hear about my new home.

"K.T.'s a real interesting place," he said. "I ain't sure yet, but I might move there myself, 'cause I'd like to have a hand in settling it. The people who live in K.T. are trying to make it a state, but they want it to be a *free* state, one where you can't own slaves. The people next door in Missouri ain't happy about it, and there's lots of fighting going on."

Kansas Territory sounded like a place I'd be happy to live in. "Tell me more about it. What does it look like?"

He said, "Where your pa's settling, it's awful flat and there ain't many trees. It's northwest of a new town called Junction City. There's plenty of buffalo and antelope, and I hear the land's good for growing corn. I'm sure you'll like it. Heck, a spunky gal like you ain't scared of rattlesnakes and windstorms and Cheyenne Indians!"

"Rattlesnakes?"

"Yep!" He grinned. "And it's adventuresome to wake up and find a tree frog on your pillow, and have mice and horned lizards everywhere."

"Horned lizards?"

"Big old lizards with horns on their heads and spikes along their sides. They won't hurt you none, even though Miz—"

He stopped.

"You said Miz again."

Rufus slapped his knee in exasperation. "Confound it if my tongue don't keep forming that word! Now, let me explain about your pa's ideas on—"

"Rufus Peacock, you tell me right now what it is you don't want to tell me about this Miz person! If you don't, I'll have a relapse and tell Aunt Laura it was your fault."

"Well . . . okay." Rufus scowled at the quilt. "But you're gonna be kinda shocked, Gilly. See, what I keep not saying is Miz Lizzie."

"Miz Lizzie? Who's that?"

"Your new stepma."

"My what?"

"Now, don't get riled up! I wasn't gonna tell you till you got stronger, but my old tongue went and got out of control, so I may as well tell you the whole story. Your pa got himself hitched proper out near Pikes Peak in a little place called Denver. That was one of the things he told you in that long letter you never got."

I let out sort of a strangled moan.

"It ain't all that bad, Gilly. Not being a marrying man myself, I can't think what possessed him to do it. But Miz Lizzie's a nice gal."

Rufus went on talking, almost faster than I could take in the words. My new stepma was named Lizzie Lincoln Bucket, and she'd been an actress in a traveling troupe. She was slender, with a mop of coal-black curls, blue eyes, and freckles on her nose. "She's a city gal, from New York," Rufus said. "She worked in a factory there, and came out to Illinois through a women's emigration society. She was hired as a seamstress, but she got tired of it pretty quick and ran off with some traveling actors that were passing through on their way out West. Your pa and I met her at a little makeshift theater in Denver. She was starring in a scene from *Romeo and Juliet*, and when your pa saw her, he said, 'Rufus, that Romeo fella can find somebody else. I'm taking Juliet for my own.' Ain't that romantic?"

"I guess," I muttered. Pa should have waited to ask me before he brought some new woman into our family. Still, Miz Lizzie did sound kind of interesting, what with being an actress and all. And I did sympathize with somebody who'd run off rather than sew all day.

Rufus said, "Anyways, Miz Lizzie and your pa fell in love, and he promised to marry her as soon as he'd found some gold. She stayed in Denver and played Juliet while your pa and I went out to seek our fortunes."

I swallowed hard. "Rufus, are you sure Pa still needs me now that he has this Lizzie woman around?"

"Still *needs* you?" he said. "Heck, yeah! Why, he loves you like an old cow loves its calf. He's proud of you, too. You should have heard him bragging on you to Miz Lizzie."

"Truly?"

"Sure as shootin'! And Miz Lizzie, she can't wait to meet you." As if sharing a secret, he leaned toward me and added, "She needs another female, such as yourself, to talk to out there on the plains. She ain't used to living out on a claim, with no people crowding around her. I think she's going to be kind of lonesome."

"Do you think she'll want me to call her Ma?" I asked Rufus.

He shook his head. "I'm sure she won't. She ain't old enough to be your ma. Besides," he added, patting the quilt over where my knee was, "there'll never be any doubt about who your real ma was. You have her smile, you know."

"I do?"

"Yep, you sure do. Your pa told me so, but I guess I ain't noticed it till now."

Aunt Laura came to the door. "Mr. Peacock, Neddy wants to know if you'll go play mumblety-peg with him and Carter. And you," she added, looking at me, "need to get some sleep."

"I don't *want* to sleep," I protested. "Did you know Pa got married again?"

My aunt replied, "Yes, Mr. Peacock told us. She sounds like a good-hearted woman, and Lord knows she'll have her hands full looking after you and that pa of yours. I *do* hope you'll give her a fair chance, and not start off feeling spiteful toward her. Now open your mouth! A nice dose of castor oil will help build up your strength."

I swallowed the castor oil without protest because my mind was on all the things Rufus had told me. They were whirling around inside my head like leaves in a windstorm.

I'd never dreamed that Pa and I would live in any place other than Prairie Flower. I *did* like the idea of living where people wanted slavery to be illegal, but I wanted to be back in Pa's and my old cabin, and play in Katy Creek, and see and do all the other things I'd been homesick for.

Then there was Miz Lizzie. My stepma. I thought about all the stepmas in the stories Granny Pea had told me. They'd been wicked, and spiteful to their stepchildren.

On the other hand, Rufus had said Miz Lizzie was lonely. I knew what it was like to be lonely. Besides, I had to admit that my skill at judging people hadn't been any too good lately. Aunt Laura, Tolliver, Clio—I'd been dead wrong about them all. I'd been wrong about David Thurmond being the Spirit, and I'd been wrong to think Dr. Granger didn't know what he was doing. I'd even been wrong about Pa—*twice*: first when I refused to believe he'd gambled away his money, and again when I thought he'd abandoned me.

"All right," I grumbled to myself. "I'll give Miz Lizzie a fair chance."

When Neddy brought my dinner, he commiserated with me about getting a stepma. "But cheer up, Gilly!" he said. "I'd be *happy* to put up with a wicked old stepma if I got to live in a place like Kansas Territory, where there's rattlesnakes and horned lizards and things. I guess you'll be rassling them like you did the bears and crocodiles in Missouri, huh?"

I didn't know how to answer. Somehow, after helping Rissy and Carrie Belle escape, I didn't have the heart for those silly boasting stories anymore.

227

"Neddy . . ." I took a deep breath. "What would you say if I told you I never actually did those things?"

His forehead wrinkled with confusion. "You mean you never twirled bears by the tails and flung tigers around and rassled crocodiles?"

"No, I'm afraid not. Missouri doesn't even *have* crocodiles or tigers or most of those other things I put in my stories. It has bears, but I never saw any."

Neddy sat on the edge of my bed and looked at the quilt. I felt lower than a groundhog's toenail, remembering all the wild, made-up stories I'd told him.

Slowly he asked me, "Would you be brave enough to fight those things if you had a chance? Like in your stories?"

I ran my finger along the edge of my dinner tray, aware of his anxious eyes on me. What could I say that wouldn't be another fib?

Thinking it out as I went, I replied, "If a bear or a tiger had you in its clutches, or a crocodile was getting set to chomp down on you, I'd do my best to save you. If that meant I had to twirl them and fling them and rassle them, I'd sure try. But I wouldn't do those things just to *do* them, without having a good reason. That wouldn't be brave; it would just be silly and showing off. Do you see what I mean?"

"I be*lieve* I do."

"Are you disappointed?"

"Some." He thought. "But I'm kind of glad, too."

"Glad?"

He nodded. "I was afraid that if I ever came to visit, you'd want *me* to fight wild animals. I was afraid you'd laugh if you found out I was scared to."

"Oh, Neddy, I'd *never* laugh at you!" I cried. "You're one of my favorite people in the whole world, and I feel truly sorry I told you fib stories. Can you forgive me?"

"I guess." He sighed sadly. "They sure were good stories, though."

"I can still tell you stories," I said, "as long as we both know they're just made up. Say, we can make up a story together!"

"Right now?"

"Sure!"

So together we concocted a story about rassling fierce horned lizards the size of cows. The story got wilder and crazier, with us riding on bears and shooting the lizards with poison arrows we got raiding a camp of Indian warriors. At the end, we flung the remaining lizards into a bottomless lake and rode home on man-eating tigers.

"That was fun!" Neddy grinned. "I like making up fib stories together."

"So do I," I said. "After I get out to K.T., we can write stories and mail them to each other. We'll write about the real-life things that happen, too, of course."

For supper that evening, I got to dress and go to the

dining room. I had to take the stairs one step at a time and stop twice to catch my breath.

"Well, it's our invalid!" Uncle Henry patted me on the back. "Good to see you looking more chipper. Sit yourself down and have some ham and fried potatoes."

As we were eating, he said, "By the way, we never did find your friend, that little wench I sold Simon Craikey. Can you believe he thought I ought to give him his money back? That conniving rascal! I always *did* say he was too hard on his people."

I stared at him.

Smooth as apple butter, Aunt Laura said, "You do have to feel sorry for Simon, having that girl get spirited away the very day after he bought her."

Uncle Henry grunted.

My aunt Laura sure beats all, I thought admiringly. I'd be pleased to have *half* as much boldness.

Now that I was able to get some exercise, I got well pretty quickly. Finally even Dr. Granger said I was ready to head West.

Rufus Peacock had one more surprise for me: we weren't going all the way to K.T. on a train. We were going most of the way on steamboats. The one we'd take down the Ohio River had velvet carpets and linen table-cloths.

"I can afford it," he said grandly. He told me how

much gold he'd found in the Rockies, and I gasped. He added, "I might buy a fancy steamboat like that myself. I've always had a hankering for one."

The day before Rufus and I were to leave, I went down to the cabins and to the kitchen to tell everybody goodbye.

Tolliver said, "You behave you'self, Miz Gilly."

"I will," I replied. Then I did something I'd never done before, for anybody: I stuck out my hand. Tolliver clasped it, and we shook.

"You better be gettin' along, li'l gal," he said. "You be careful out where you's goin'. Don't you get et up by no wildcats or nothin'."

"You be careful, too, Tolliver," I replied. I felt my eyes tearing up, so I turned and ran back to the house.

I made one last trip to the river. I wasn't strong enough yet to scramble up onto my branch, so I leaned against the tree and looked out over the water. It seemed like a coon's age since I'd stood here and hugged Rissy and Carrie Belle goodbye. I wondered whether they were in Canada yet, and whether Rissy's leg had healed, and whether she would be lucky, like me, and find her pa.

In the morning, Aunt Laura gave me several envelopes full of herb seeds.

"Thank you," I said. "I'll raise them carefully, I promise. Aunt Laura—"

"Yes?"

I blurted out, "I'm not happy about going to a new place and having a stepma."

She nodded. "It'll be a big change for you, Mary Gillian. But even though you have your faults, you're not one to run away from a challenge. Besides, those people in Kansas Territory need you. I doubt they have a good herbalist to care for them. And," she added slowly, "I hear that it's quite an up-and-coming place. I believe it even has a *rail*road! I'm sure someone with your spirit will be quite useful there."

A railroad? My spirit? Of course! She meant that those freedom-loving people in K.T. had an underground railroad to help slaves from Missouri escape!

"I'll do all I can to help," I promised Aunt Laura.

"Good! And—uh," she added stiffly, "before you go, you might jot down some of your remedies for me. That one for spicebush tea and some of the others you mentioned. They sound like they might be worth trying. And I'll give you some of my recipes."

"Okay." I held off until she'd walked away before I broke into a big smile.

While we waited for Jupiter to bring the wagon around, I wrote down all of Granny Pea's best remedy recipes.

"Much obliged," my aunt said when I gave them to her. "Here are my best ones."

"Thank you." I opened my mouth and closed it again. I knew that if I told her I was proud to be kin to her, she'd turn red with embarrassment and not know what to say.

"Did you want something else?" she asked.

I shook my head.

"Then we'd best hurry. Jupiter has already loaded the bags onto the wagon."

Outside, I kissed her on the cheek and exchanged polite hugs with Uncle Henry.

"Have a good trip, Gilly," he said.

"Yes, sir, and thank you for letting me stay here." I wanted to add, *I hope someday you'll see how wrong it is to own another human being*, but I figured it would be better if I hoped it silently.

When it was time to tell Neddy goodbye, the tears started rolling down my cheeks. I couldn't help it. Neddy got all teary-eyed as well, and we hugged each other so hard we lost our balance and fell over into Aunt Laura's peony bushes. Everybody laughed, and Uncle Henry helped us up. Neddy and I hugged each other more sedately and shyly kissed each other's cheeks. I climbed onto the wagon seat beside Rufus and Jupiter, and dried my eyes with David Thurmond's handkerchief.

Then, just as Jupiter was getting set to slap the reins, I cried, "Wait a minute! I forgot something!"

The menfolk groaned, and Aunt Laura rolled her eyes.

I didn't care, though. I had to go back inside for a minute, because I'd just thought of how to tell Aunt Laura what I wanted to tell her.

I ran into the house, up the steps, and into my aunt and uncle's bedroom. Carefully I lifted the forget-me-not pendant over my head. I held it against my cheek for a moment.

After all, it's not the only thing I have of Ma's, I told myself. *I have her smile.*

"Gilly, are you coming?" Uncle Henry yelled.

"Be right there!"

Quickly I laid the pendant on Aunt Laura's pillow. Then I ran downstairs to start my new life.